PENGUIN CANADA

THE SINGING STONE

O.R. Melling was born in Ireland and grew up in Toronto with her seven sisters and two brothers. She has a B.A. in philosophy and Celtic Studies from Trinity College at the University of Toronto, and an M.A. in mediaeval Irish history. At present, she lives in Ireland with her daughter, Findabhair.

Also by O.R. Melling

The Druid's Tune

My Blue Country

The Chronicles of Faerie

The Hunter's Moon

The Summer King

The Light-Bearer's Daughter

The Book of Dreams

Adult Fiction

Falling Out of Time

the Singing Stone

O.R. Melling

PENGUIN CANADA

Published by the Penguin Group

Penguin Group (Canada), 90 Eglinton Avenue East, Suite 700, Toronto, Ontario, Canada M4P 2Y3
    (a division of Pearson Canada Inc.)

Penguin Group (USA) Inc., 375 Hudson Street, New York, New York 10014, U.S.A.
Penguin Books Ltd, 80 Strand, London WC2R 0RL, England
Penguin Ireland, 25 St Stephen's Green, Dublin 2, Ireland (a division of Penguin Books Ltd)
Penguin Group (Australia), 250 Camberwell Road, Camberwell, Victoria 3124, Australia
    (a division of Pearson Australia Group Pty Ltd)
Penguin Books India Pvt Ltd, 11 Community Centre, Panchsheel Park, New Delhi – 110 017, India
Penguin Group (NZ), cnr Airborne and Rosedale Roads, Albany, Auckland 1310, New Zealand
    (a division of Pearson New Zealand Ltd)
Penguin Books (South Africa) (Pty) Ltd, 24 Sturdee Avenue, Rosebank, Johannesburg 2196,
    South Africa

Penguin Group, Registered Offices: 80 Strand, London WC2R 0RL, England

First published by Viking Kestrel, Canada, 1986
Published by Puffin Books, Canada, 1988
Published in Penguin Canada paperback by Penguin Group (Canada),
    a division of Pearson Canada Inc., 2004

(WEB)   10 9 8 7 6 5 4 3 2

NATIONAL LIBRARY OF CANADA CATALOGUING IN PUBLICATION

Melling, O. R.
    The singing stone / O.R. Melling.

Originally published: Markham, Ont. : Viking Kestrel, 1986.
ISBN 0-14-301667-9

I. Title.

PS8576.E463S5 2004   jC813'.54   C2003-904862-4

Visit the Penguin Group (Canada) website at **www.penguin.ca**

Special and corporate bulk purchase rates available; please see
www.penguin.ca/corporatesales or call 1-800-399-6858, ext. 477 or 474

In memory of my Uncle Frank
who took me through the mountains
in search of the dolmen and bluebells...

ACKNOWLEDGEMENTS

THANK YOU TO FINDABHAIR AS ALWAYS for her advice and encouragement, Georgie Whelan for so much, Charles Halpern and Nicholas Staines who were kidnapped for the story, Nena Hardie dear friend and host in Toronto, Senior Editor Barb Berson, former editor and publisher Cynthia Good, Jennifer Handel for overseeing the book, Cathy MacLean for art design and all the helpful people at Penguin, my agents Lynn and David Bennett of the Transatlantic Literary Agency Inc., the Arts Council of Ireland for a Travel Grant, Bray Urban District Council and Wicklow County Council for arts awards, the Cultural Relations Committee of the Department of Arts, Sport and Tourism (Ireland) for travel funding, and the Canadian Children's Book Centre for their continuing support through the years.

Thanks also to Claire Tuffy and the Commissioners of Public Works, Eire, for special entrance to Newgrange/the *Brugh na Boinne*.

The truth was not known beneath
the sky of stars,
Whether they were of heaven or of earth.

Lebor Gabala

PART ONE

THE QUEST

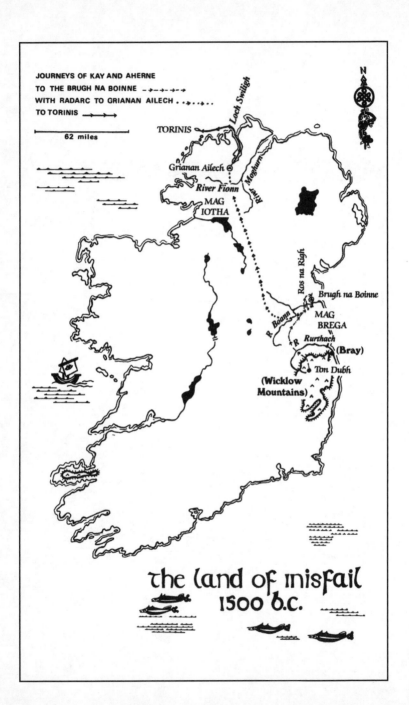

JOURNEYS OF KAY AND AHERNE
TO THE BRUGH NA BOINNE – ∗ – ∗ – ∗ – ∗ →
WITH RADARC TO GRIANAN AILECH . . ∗ . . ∗ . .
TO TORINIS →→→→

62 miles

Loch Swilligh

TORINIS

Grianan Ailech

River Fionn

MAG
IOTHA

Mogharn River

Ros na Righ

Brugh na Boinne

MAG
BREGA

R Boann

R
R Rurthach
(Bray)

Ton Dubh

(Wicklow
Mountains)

the land of inisfail
1500 b.c.

CHAPTER ONE

T<small>HE OLD APARTMENT</small> building stood on a quiet lonely street, like a secluded monastery set in the heart of the city. Its stone walls were dark and scarred with age, looking down on a paved courtyard and a small pool that gleamed with moonlight. The night was warm with the breath of a midsummer's breeze. In the shadow of the walls a great oak tree rustled gracefully.

A lone figure crouched at the edge of the pool, a young girl with blonde hair that fell over her shoulders. She wore a woollen shawl draped around her nightgown and her feet were bare. As she leaned over the pool, her features were reflected in the water; a narrow face, vague and lost in thought, and grey eyes that shone as pale as her hair.

Kay Warrick had been awakened from a dream. The same dream which had come to her again and again that past month.

'Who's calling me?' she whispered. 'How can I answer if I don't know?'

She trailed her hand in the pool. As the ripples disturbed her reflection, she recalled the other face, the one in her dream. A beautiful woman with hair streaming like fire and eyes that glittered like emerald stones. The face was offset by visions of madness, a riot of colour, things falling apart, bursting open, like fireworks or explosions. Was that an antlered figure behind her or did she have antlers herself? There was no form to the dream but it conveyed a clear and undeniable message. A wild cry of the heart and mind. A cry for help.

Kay wasn't frightened by nightmares. Strange dreams and images had haunted her throughout her young life. It was part of the great mystery of her existence, a mystery she had only begun to unravel.

'Everything all right?' came a voice beside her.

Kay jumped up in fright, nearly falling into the pool in her haste. A hand reached out to steady her, then withdrew again as she let out a cry.

'Sorry to startle you,' the young man said quickly. 'I'm Alan Manduca. I live in the building. I'm just getting home from a late night at the library.'

As if to confirm his words, he shifted the books that were cradled under his arm.

Though she didn't return his smile, Kay calmed down when she recognized him. A student at the university. She had often passed him in the hall on her way to work and he always said hello. A foreigner, judging by his accent and looks, he had a pleasant handsome face. It was squarish and strong-featured with dark eyes and dark complexion. His build was stocky and he stood with legs apart, confident and unshakeable. She could sense in his stance and the steady gaze of his eyes a certain strength of character.

Alan in turn was appraising Kay. He had been aware of her for some time as she tended to dress in a quixotic fashion, long skirts and vivid blouses, with bracelets and earrings that tinkled like a wind chime. She looked like a gypsy despite her fair colouring. And that peculiar look which seemed to come from behind her grey eyes instead of looking at you directly. At first glance she appeared frail and waif-like but there was also about her an aloof and independent air.

'You'll catch cold,' he said in a deliberately friendly voice, pointing to her bare feet.

Kay shrugged and didn't answer him. Images were forming in her mind, like pictures dancing in a mirror, and she knew somehow that they belonged to Alan. These kinds of images had come to her since she was a child but they still unsettled her. Like an invasion of her thoughts, they appeared and disappeared without her consent or control. In this case, however, the images were pleasing.

An island in a blue, sun-warmed sea. A man riding his horse by the shore. The rider wore a white tunic over shining mail and his shield was emblazoned with an eight-pointed cross.

'Do you come from an island country?' Kay asked Alan abruptly.

He looked surprised but answered with a quick nod.

'I'm from Malta.'

'Makes sense,' Kay murmured. At least she could figure that one out. The images were often incomprehensible. She guessed that it was Alan's ancestry she had seen and she was pleased to think of him as coming from a line of knights or kings perhaps. She was beginning to like him.

'I'm going to an island tomorrow,' she said. 'To Ireland.'

'Off on holidays?' he asked.

'No, not holidays,' and she frowned as she thought of her reason for going. 'It's a long story,' she said uneasily.

'I'd like to hear it,' Alan said, seeing his chance. 'But you shouldn't stay out here. Why don't you throw on some clothes and come over to my apartment for a cup of tea?'

Kay's frown deepened and he added quickly, 'I'm perfectly trustworthy, believe me. I come from a good family—'

'I know,' Kay said, interrupting him with a little laugh. She did feel she could trust him and she really wanted, needed to talk to someone. 'What's your apartment number?'

'And what's your name?' he asked when he had told her.

By the time Kay arrived at Alan's door, he had made the pot of tea and set it out on the coffee table with sugar and milk. She took the cup he offered her and curled up in the one big armchair in the room. Around her were shelves of books, a desk cluttered with papers, and an old sofa on which Alan was now reclining.

'What do you study?' she asked him.

'Political Science,' he said. 'Rather boring, I'm afraid. How to govern and misgovern. I'm just finishing my Master's thesis. But you're going to tell me about your trip,' he prompted.

Kay sighed. Where to begin so that it wouldn't sound ridiculous?

'I'm an orphan,' she said bluntly with a trace of defiance.

Alan raised his eyebrows at her tone but remained silent. 'I was in an institution when I was very little and then I was fostered out from home to home. Some were good. Some weren't.' She shrugged painfully. 'I was never adopted. Too strange, I guess.' She added these last words more for herself than for him. She was already sifting the information she would give him. She decided to leave out the part about the dreams and images. 'My last foster-mother wrote to the orphanage to see if she could discover anything about my history. But there was nothing to find. I was an abandoned baby. Really and truly left on the doorstep.' Again the pained shrug.

Alan was listening intently and watching Kay's expressions as she spoke. His interest was sincere and he added the occasional 'hmm' to encourage her past the difficult parts.

'My last foster-mother was the best, actually, but I left her when I turned sixteen. I was fed up with living in other people's homes. So I got a job and moved out on my own. I thought that was it, you know? Look after myself, grow up or whatever. Then early last year . . .'

She paused, suddenly afraid to tell him what had happened. It seemed too absurd to relate. And kept to herself it was perhaps more real. Alan made one of his encouraging noises and she continued. 'I got this parcel in the post. No letter. No return address. But it was definitely for me. A parcel of books. Eighteen in all, which is the age I'm supposed to be. Funny coincidence, eh?' She lifted her hands in a gesture of disbelief. 'They're very old books, some falling apart, with worn leather covers and fancy print. It was kind of nice, really. A surprise gift from nowhere. But who sent them?

'Most of them are in English. Lovely stories, legends and fairy tales from all over Europe. But some are written in a language I couldn't recognize at first. I took one of the books to the library and an old guy there told me it looked like Gaelic. He said I should contact a language professor at the university. So I did and . . .' Kay started to laugh. 'I spent the year learning *Old Irish,* believe it or not.'

'At the university?' Alan said.

'Nah,' said Kay. 'I didn't finish high school. But the professor was really nice and she lent me a stack of dictionaries and grammars. I taught myself.' She smiled proudly. 'I spent this year translating the Irish books. Did them all. I'm quite good at it now.'

'Well done,' Alan murmured admiringly. Then he shook his head. 'But what does it mean?'

Kay slapped the arm of her chair. 'Exactly my question!' A pensive look came over her face. 'Though the stories are from different countries, they're all about the same thing. And the Irish books made that clear to me. It was like wandering through a maze. Each story is set around these ancient stone monuments—some of the English books call them megaliths. Tombs and stonehenges and stuff like that. And then, at the heart of every story, is something called "The Singing Stone." It holds the answer to every mystery.'

Alan's eyes widened. Kay saw the doubt in his look as he began to wonder if she was spinning him an elaborate yarn.

'One story was set in Malta,' she told him, hoping to regain his confidence. 'It was about a stone temple.'

Alan's doubts disappeared as he nodded with excitement.

'Yes, we have megaliths too, though few people know about them. Very old and beautiful temples. I used to play in them when I was a kid.'

Another coincidence? Kay thought to herself. She almost told him, then, about her dreams and the strange images that came into her mind when she was awake. What a relief it would be to share that secret with someone. She was tired of keeping everything to herself, never knowing what anything meant, forever wondering why she was so different. But her chance passed by as Alan suddenly decided that they should have some toast and a fresh pot of tea.

Kay watched as he bustled around the small kitchen, plugging in the toaster and putting the kettle on to boil. He apologized for the lack of jam and biscuits, all the time bemoaning the life of the poor student. Kay found herself laughing with him. She was enjoying herself thoroughly. This late-night visit was something new for her. She had never had any friends, male or female. She was always too shy and withdrawn. Too strange. She changed her mind again about the dreams and images. She would definitely *not* tell him. He had been kind enough to believe the rest of her story and she couldn't bring herself to test him further.

Alan offered her the plate of buttered toast and poured out their tea. Then he sat down again with a completely absorbed look.

'This is truly amazing,' he said seriously. 'Do you think the books might have something to do with your past? Maybe someone has sent them to you as a kind of clue you're to follow? Like in a mystery story?'

Kay munched quietly on her toast, too nervous to speak at first. He had expressed her innermost hope and again she felt it might lose its reality if she said it out loud.

'That is what I believe,' she managed to say at last. 'And that's why I'm going to Ireland. The stories all point to the Singing Stone and it's supposed to be standing somewhere in that country. Crazy as it sounds, I'm going to look for it.'

Alan was quiet for a while as he mulled over everything she had told him. It was all rather incredible and yet he couldn't deny the logic of her decision. He would do the same thing himself, given the circumstances, no matter how mad it appeared. A wild goose chase? With a pang of sympathy he looked closely at the girl, at her thin face and pale eyes.

'But really,' he said with a flush of anger. 'I'd like to know who sent you those books. If they wanted you to go off to Ireland on this search, why didn't they just come out and tell you? What kind of game are they playing? I think it's rather cruel.'

Alan stopped speaking. His emotions were running high, tangled up with this girl who had been a stranger only a short time before. He shook his head. 'There are some very strange people in this world.'

'Yes, there are,' Kay murmured.

She grew aware of the lateness of the night, and she felt drained after revealing so much. She stood up with a slow graceful movement.

'I have to go now. My plane leaves early tomorrow. Thanks so much for the tea and toast and all.'

Alan stood up too. Of the same height, they gazed into each other's eyes.

'You're a courageous woman,' he said with genteel formality. He kissed her on the cheek. 'I wish you a safe and successful journey.'

As he opened the door for her, he asked hopefully, 'Are you coming back here?'

'In a month,' Kay answered with a shy smile.

'Let me know when you do,' he said, and he grinned. 'I want to hear the rest of the story.'

Chapter Two

As the train pulled out of the station, leaving Dublin city in its wake, Kay sat back in her seat with a sigh of relief. She had survived her first flight on an airplane and had managed without too much difficulty to tote her luggage from airport to bus and bus station to train. She was now well on her way to the small town where the travel agent had booked her a month's stay in a boarding house.

Any doubts and fears that Kay had about arriving in a strange country began to dissipate as she stared at the scenery that swept past her window. She was journeying along the eastern coast of Ireland and beyond her spread the Irish Sea. Green waves glimmered in the light of a summer's day beneath a sky drifting with clouds. Rising above the water's edge were the hills and mountains of Wicklow. They shadowed the train as it wound its way along the cliffs, occasionally opening to a dark, noisy tunnel.

Green was the colour of the countryside, from the fields and hills that rolled along the horizon to the hedges that grew over the walls of every station stop. Having lived her life in a grey city, Kay was overcome by the bright beauty of the landscape. She felt it beckoning to her with warmth and promise.

'Is this my homeland?' she mused to herself. 'Or the country of my parents perhaps?'

Kay's eyes settled on the suitcase which contained her books. Could ancient stories answer those questions? She remembered Alan's suggestion. Was this a cruel game someone was playing on her?

It can't be, she reassured herself. There's too much to be discovered. Where did I come from? Why do I have strange dreams and pictures in my mind? The books are part of a whole puzzle and there must be an explanation.

In all the stories the Singing Stone held the answers to every question. It made sense that it would hold the answer to hers.

'Please let me find you,' Kay whispered as the Irish country-side sped past her.

Bray was the place where Kay had chosen to stay, a small seaside town with the Wicklow mountains at its back. Sea and mountain. These two were always present in the stories about the Stone. With the help of maps she had drawn herself, Kay was convinced that it was the Irish Sea and the Wicklow mountains to which the stories referred. Bray was therefore an ideal place to begin her search.

The boarding house where she would live that month was one of a long row of Bed & Breakfasts overlooking the sea front. As soon as Kay moved in, she unpacked the guides she had brought to help her search. Maps of Wicklow were pinned over the flowered wallpaper. Her drawings and papers were scattered around the room: over the big bed with its lumpy mattress; in front of the old fireplace with its blue-gas fire; on top of the wooden dresser and mirrored wardrobe. Spilling over the floor in disorderly tiers were her special books, earmarked and well-thumbed, with notes written in the margins and paragraphs underlined.

'A student, are ye?' the landlady asked when she came to check on Kay.

'Sort of,' Kay mumbled in reply.

'Dinner's at half-six, love. Don't be late. I've the house full and first served is best fed, as I always say. Ye could do with a bit of nourishment,' she added, frowning at Kay's thinness.

Kay smiled at the landlady's own portly figure and promised she wouldn't be late.

It's nice that she cares, Kay thought to herself as she unpacked the last of her clothes. I think I'm going to like this place.

Kay spent her first days in Ireland recovering from jet lag and wandering around the town of Bray. She was eager to begin her search for the Stone but she had no intention of racing off without knowing for certain where she was going. She had spent too much time, money and effort preparing for this trip and she would not ruin her chances by chasing a blind lead.

Her maps were marked and circled with various journeys she could take through the mountains, and yet she knew somehow that only one path would lead her to what she sought. She began to read her books again, seeking frantically for clues, but when she stared in desperation at her maps, each journey seemed as likely as the next. How could she know which one to take? Then one night the dream which had tormented her in Canada came back in full force.

The images were no longer fragmented but stark and potently clear. A mountain peak. A stormy sky. A woman standing beneath a massive archway of stone. Her long red hair flew wildly in the wind. Her face was fierce and tragic. A green cloak swirled about her, the same shining colour as her eyes. It seemed to Kay that the emerald eyes pierced the veil of the dream and settled directly on *her*.

Kay woke with a start and sat up in bed. The room was dark. A violent wind rattled the old sashes of the window. Rain splattered against the panes. She could hear the roar of the waves echoing from the sea front. It wasn't a night for rambling but the intensity of the dream demanded action. With trembling fingers she pulled on jeans and boots, sweater and raincoat. Then she crept quietly out of the house and headed down to the sea shore.

It was a wild night. The elements raged. Nature sang with the fullness of its power. The sea, like a great leviathan unchained, was heaving itself over the sea wall with savage abandon. The sky, a dark tempest, silver-edged and moon-clouded, was hurling rain downward to match the watery outburst below.

'As above, so below,' Kay murmured. It was a phrase repeated often in her books.

Her excitement was rising. She knew something was up. She could feel it drawing near, whatever it was.

She walked along the promenade, a pale pathway of stone that bordered the strand. As the waves crashed over the metal railings and down onto the pavement, she stepped in a careful dance to avoid the fury of the water. She had begun to sepa-rate the sounds of the night—the rush of wind, the roar of waves, the lash of rain—when she heard a new voice in the resounding chorus. Standing still and alert, she finally found its origin. As the waves tore up the pebbly shore and surged against the promenade, small stones were flung upon the ground, landing with the clip-clopping music of a horse on cobblestones.

Gifts from the sea, Kay thought with delight.

When she looked down at the sea-flung stones she realized her words were true. Kay caught her breath as she stared at the smooth pebbles that sprayed the pavement like stars. Wet and glistening, they formed an unmistakable pattern. A triple spiral whirling outward.

Kay almost cried out as she recognized the sign. She had drawn it herself on one of her maps, the outline of a trek through mountain and valley, one of the possible paths she could take in search of the Stone.

She looked around her, at the dark sky and the wind-driven sea.

'Thank you!' she shouted into the storm. 'Whoever, whatever, thank you!'

Though thoroughly drenched and chilled to the bone, Kay hurried back to the house with a light heart. She was now certain of the journey she must take and she would set out that very morning.

As she turned on the gas fire and scrambled under the rough warm blankets of her bed, a fiery image rose in her mind. A great stone archway and a majestic woman in wind-tossed cloak. Kay shivered as much from anticipation as from the cold. They had joined together, her dreams and her search. Once again, everything pointed to the Singing Stone and she was on the road to its discovery.

*   *   *

'Here ye are, love. Enniskerry,' the conductor called out.

Kay thanked him and stepped from the bus, shifting her backpack till it settled comfortably on her shoulders. She wore a bulky sweater and high rubber boots over her blue jeans. In her backpack were a groundsheet, sandwiches and a flask of tea, her maps, a compass and a box of matches. She would have taken her books if they hadn't been too heavy.

'Off to the Arctic?' the landlady had said when Kay was leaving the house.

'I'll be gone for a while,' Kay had replied, realizing that she had no idea for how long.

What if I get lost? Kay thought now, as she began the long walk out of Enniskerry village up into the mountains. Who would know? And who would care?

She pushed the gloomy thoughts out of her mind. She had not travelled all the way to Ireland to be turned back by fear or worry.

Kay's map described the route she was to take. The arms of the triple spiral reached out from Enniskerry to the north, south and west. It was a ritual walk, like the ones mentioned in some of her stories, and she traced the pattern faithfully.

Hour after hour she marched: over piebald peaks coloured with purple heather and yellow gorse; down into wild valleys tangled with green fern and moistened by the amber flow of the Glencree River; through spinneys of old and young trees, brown pine needles crunching underfoot.

As time passed her senses grew confused. Buffeted by the winds of the uplands, blinded by the dappled light of the river glen, smothered by the scent of green profusion, she wandered in a daze. The shadows of the trees were in her eyes, the silence of the hills was in her heart. Already she was moving into time-less space as the endless flow of life eddied around her like a deep pool.

She stopped at intervals to rest and eat but she didn't linger, keeping up a steady pace throughout the day. Though dusk was descending over the hills and her feet and legs were tired, she pressed on to the final stage of her journey.

Twilight brought her a world of grey haze. In the shifting mood of light, the mountains glowed in washed smudges of blue and mauve. Across the pale sky birds were flying home in the evening, the shape of seven marking the drifts of cloud like an omen.

Kay was now completing the last arm of the spiral, wandering westward in the waning light. She grew uneasy as the way became more difficult in the dimness. It seemed that the landscape itself was beginning to defy her. She was being led into the furthest and most desolate reaches of the mountains and the path was ever steeper and more treacherous. A reddish water seeped from the ground as if the hillsides were wounded and bleeding. The wind whistled through dark and eyeless spaces. Dusk gave way to night as a pall of gloom fell over the mountains.

Kay shivered fitfully as she walked. A cheerful memory flashed through her mind; the warm glow of the lamp in Alan's apartment and a plate of buttered toast with tea. In that moment she felt the utter loneliness of her journey and wondered why it had to be this way. With sad eyes she looked up at the still white stars and shining moon.

'I wish I had a companion,' she said with a little sigh.

Now the doubts began to assail her. Why was she roaming alone at night through the mountains of a foreign countryside? What if it was all a huge mistake? Maybe one of her many foster-parents had sent her the books as a present but forgot to enclose a letter? Maybe she had let her imagination run away with her, finding clues that weren't really there.

Kay stopped in her tracks as the worst thought of all weighed down upon her. Perhaps they were just fairy tales after all. *Perhaps she was searching for something that didn't exist.*

It took all Kay's willpower not to cry at that moment. The cold dark of night seemed to press against her on all sides. She felt lost and hopeless.

She had come to a sharp ledge higher than all the others she had climbed. Even in the darkness she could see the tangle of brambles and gorse that barred her way. Why bother to go any further? Why scale another height, knowing that she would find nothing beyond it? All the walking she had done that day, all the endless meandering through hill and valley. Senseless. Useless. Why suffer more?

It was like this in the stories, Kay reminded herself with effort. The heroes wandered lost in the wilderness. It was one of the tests they had to pass before they found what they were looking for.

She stared grimly at the ledge. It would be difficult but if she held on to the brambles no matter how much they scratched her, she could manage to climb up without falling.

'I've only been wandering for a day,' she told herself. 'Maybe it's supposed to take longer. I'll just have to keep going.'

Before her doubts could overwhelm her again, Kay clambered up the ledge. Fighting for toeholds and clinging painfully to the thorn bushes, she moved slowly upwards. Her breath came in short gasps as she struggled. The air seemed thinner the higher she climbed, but still she continued. At last she reached the summit.

Prepared to find nothing and ready to move onwards, Kay stood shocked by the scene before her.

She had found one of the high hidden pastures that only the mountain sheep normally tread. It was flooded with moonlight, a silver bowl set in the dark rim of the mountains. A bluish mist issued from the ground like the breath of the earth. But it wasn't the eerie beauty of the meadow that shocked Kay, it was the sight of the megalith that loomed before her.

Stone upon stone it stood, a massive dolmen, a colossal archway. Stark and ancient, it towered against the sky, dwarfing the muted shapes and shadows of the meadow. Though made of stone it gleamed with a dark metallic sheen which reinforced the impression that it was a giant doorway.

Kay stared at the awesome sight with a mixture of joy and horror. Here before her stood the greatest of the megaliths. The Stone that answered all questions. The goal of her dreams and strivings. And she wasn't ready for it. Alone in that silent field, high in the lost reaches of the mountains, she felt her will weaken as she faced the ancient giant.

Would she have to approach it? Was it *really* the Singing Stone? Why did it stand so dark and silent? Like a tomb. Would it hurt her? Would it sing? What now?

For one long moment Kay actually considered turning back. She was shaking with terror. Perhaps it was better to muddle along with uncertainty? Maybe she didn't need her questions answered.

'But I want the answers,' she argued with herself. 'I want to know who I am and where I come from.'

Tired of her battle with doubts and fears, and exhausted from the long march of the day, Kay surrendered quietly to her own desire. With head held high and fists clenched against the unknown, she walked slowly towards the dolmen and passed under its arch.

CHAPTER THREE

F̲OR A SECOND ONLY KAY STOOD beneath the Stone, but in that moment she heard a note of music so pure, so exquisite that her whole being thrilled to the sound. Then, as if some invisible hand had given her a light but irresistible push, she found herself on the other side of the archway.

Kay saw immediately that she was in a different place. Though the starry night still shone above her and the same mountains shadowed the landscape, she now faced a vast and impenetrable forest. The peak on which she stood was but a small island cresting the sea of tall pine and gnarled oak. The great trees whispered in the night wind, an insistent sighing that refused any denial of their presence.

Kay whirled around to seek the shelter of the dolmen, but found herself staring into empty space with more woods beyond. The Stone was gone. Fear and wonder coursed through her and she sat down weakly on the ground and hugged her backpack to her chest.

Her mind spun crazily, trying to make sense of something that was not sensible, till she began to talk quietly to herself.

'Okay, I've been ignoring this all along and now I can't anymore. This is not a normal situation and I'm not a normal person. Normal people do not get moving pictures in their minds. Nor do they get messages from dreams and pebbles thrown out of the sea. And they certainly don't receive strange books from nowhere that send them off to other countries looking for singing stones. Either I accept all of this as true for me or I go insane. It's that simple.'

It was that simple but still it wasn't easy. Another thought struck Kay and she sat up straight as she considered it. This might not be a normal situation in the modern world but it was in fact very like the stories in her books. Except in this case she herself appeared to be the heroine. It was an uncomfortable thought in some ways, but it did make sense of everything that was happening to her.

I hope I'm strong enough, she thought as she remembered the hardships those other heroes had endured.

But indeed she felt stronger already. With this new understanding she accepted the idea that some great adventure lay ahead and she was determined to face it as best she could.

'I guess the Stone was the beginning of the journey and not the end,' she said to herself. 'Or else everything that happens from now on *is* the answer I'm looking for.'

She shook her head in confusion. No use racing in circles and trying to figure things out. Better to take the adventure as it came.

Kay opened her backpack and pulled out the groundsheet and matches. She had to get through the night and she intended to make herself comfortable. She collected wood from the fringes of the forest to build a camp fire. As the flames rose to warm and cheer her, she stared at the dark trees that lay just beyond.

Was it dangerous here? Should she sleep or not? She was still debating the matter when she heard a rustling noise at the edge of the forest. Her body stiffened with alarm. A thin shape was creeping through the undergrowth. Kay peered anxiously into the dense trees, trying to sift branch and trunk from shape and shadow. There it was again. She caught her breath. A small white face was looking out at her, framed by leaves. And two round eyes, wild with fright.

Kay moved on impulse. She jumped up and raced towards the spot. Crashing through the undergrowth, she grabbed hold of the tiny creature before it could flee. There was a brief struggle as small fists beat vainly on her head and chest, then she dragged the screeching bundle out of the bushes and up to the camp fire.

'Now then,' said Kay, breathless but holding tight, 'who are you and what do you want? Are you a boy or a girl?'

It looked like a child, so frail and small, with bare feet and coloured rags for clothing. The hair was short and jagged as if sheared with a blunt instrument, but by the firelight it shone a rich hue of red-gold. The face upturned to Kay was one of startling beauty yet there was something very wrong with it. The features were gaunt and hollow, their sickly pallor accentuated by the eyes that glittered with a frenzied look.

Pity welled up in Kay and she spoke in a soothing tone. 'It's okay, I won't hurt you.'

As the green eyes stared back at her blankly, Kay started with surprise. Red hair and green eyes! The woman in her dreams? But so utterly different! Acting on a hunch, Kay spoke slowly in the language she had worked so hard to learn.

'I won't hurt you,' she repeated in Old Irish. 'Kay is my name. Will you tell me yours?'

The ragged girl lost her frightened look once she understood Kay's words, but her eyes were still wary.

'That is all I can tell you,' she whispered, 'for I know little else but my name. I am Aherne.'

Kay let go of the girl now that they were talking but Aherne crouched by the fire as if she were a prisoner. Kay herself sat in a kind of daze. If Aherne was the woman in her dreams, then Kay was linked to her in some way. And speaking in Old Irish! That could only mean . . . Kay's mind threatened her with insanity again, but she fought for control. This was not a normal situation. She had already accepted that. And here was something new to accept. If they were speaking Old Irish, she could be nowhere but in Ireland's past. The ancient, ancient past.

'Are you a Druid?' Aherne asked fearfully, breaking the silence at last. 'I saw you appear on the hill as if out of air. And why do you wear such strange garb?'

Kay remembered the Druids in her Irish stories. They were priests and magicians who had special powers.

'I'm not a Druid,' she answered truthfully, 'but I did just appear here. I can't explain it and it's hard to believe, but I come from a different time and place. Far in the future.'

A tremor of awe ran through Aherne but there was also a flash of hope in her eyes. 'Have you come to help me?'

'Maybe,' Kay said uncertainly. 'That could be why I'm here. I saw you in my dreams and I knew you were asking for help. But that wasn't why I . . .'

Aherne's face twisted with emotion as she interrupted Kay's speech.

'The Goddess heard me! I have been crying and crying for help. Days, perhaps weeks, I have wandered lost in the forest. My mind is all but broken. I do not know who I am or even who my parents are but this I do know—something terrible hangs over me. Some doom or curse that I have forgotten. And the rising shadow of the future has all but dimmed my past.'

Kay listened to the girl with sympathy.

'We're the same that way,' she said softly to Aherne. 'I don't know my past either. I guess that's why we've met. We obviously belong together somehow.'

Aherne's worn face brightened at this but Kay found herself frowning in return. She could see that the younger girl already looked up to her, and no doubt expected her to be the leader in whatever they should do next. Accustomed to being on her own, Kay did not like the idea of taking responsibility for someone else. Especially a lost and ragtaggle child. Kay sighed ruefully as she remembered that she had wished for a companion. There was no use complaining now that she had one.

'Can you remember anything?' she asked the girl. 'I mean, do you know where we are or anything about this place?'

Aherne nodded eagerly. 'It is only my own history that fails me. I know my tribe and the history of my land. This is the isle of Inisfail and my people are the Tuatha De Danaan, the tribe of the Goddess Danu. Do you know of us?'

Kay grew thoughtful as she recalled the stories in her Irish books. Vague memories, certain knowledge and a dark foreboding crowded her mind. The Tuatha De Danaan. There was a tragic story attached to this race.

'I know legends about your people,' Kay said, 'but since I'm travelling backwards in time I can't be sure where or when I've landed.' She shook her head. 'This is hopeless. A real case of the blind leading the blind. We need someone to tell us what's going on.' Kay rested her head in her hand and stared into the fire. 'There was a wise man in one of my stories. What was his name? "One of True Knowledge," he was called. Tuan?'

'Fintan Tuan?' Aherne said with surprise. 'Surely not him. The madman of the mountains?'

22

She started to laugh. The sudden gaiety eased the lines in her face so that she looked young and spirited despite her gauntness.

Kay noticed the change and felt a pang of relief. So the girl had strength of her own. She might not be as helpless as Kay feared.

'Well, even if he is crazy,' Kay said with a grin, 'he still might be able to help us. I mean, what else can we do? Where else can we go?'

Aherne sobered immediately as she saw the sense in Kay's words.

'They say he lives in these mountains,' she said seriously. 'In a high eyrie between the peaks of Ton Dubh, beyond the River Glancrigh.'

'Good. If he's not too far away, he's definitely our best bet,' Kay said. 'We'll go looking for him first thing tomorrow.' She was happy now that they had some direction, no matter how tenuous. 'In the meantime, let's try and get some sleep.'

The two girls gathered more wood and settled down for the night beside their camp fire. The ground was hard and cold but they built a shelter of branches against the wind and used Kay's groundsheet as a makeshift mattress.

As Aherne curled up to sleep, she laid her small hand on Kay's arm.

'I am glad you are here,' she whispered. 'I have been so alone and frightened.'

Aherne fell asleep soon after, but Kay remained awake. She was touched by Aherne's words but they brought home to her once more that she was in some way responsible for the girl. It was not a duty she wanted, but she could hardly refuse to help her now that they were together.

Kay watched the fire as it crackled and burned. The night hung over her like a black veil threaded darker still with the inky lace of the forest. Her thoughts circled confusedly in her mind. The story was changing. Kay had understood that she was searching for *her* past, the answers to *her* questions, but now she was linked with another who was searching too. Kay turned to look at the girl who slept beside her. The flickering light of the fire illumined Aherne's features. She could be no more than fourteen and yet even in sleep her face was marked with hardship. Why such trials for one so young?

Kay had never tried to make the pictures come into her mind. They were something which made her different and she had always hoped they would go away. But now for the first time in her life it occurred to her that they might be useful. If she could call up images from Aherne, she might find out why the girl had lost her memory. Not really knowing what to do or whether such an effort would work, Kay concentrated on the girl beside her. Only when she began to succeed with her approach did Kay consider the possibility that it might be dangerous. From her own dreams she knew that the sleeping mind was unstable, a fathomless pool of submerged and chaotic images. But it was too late to stop. A picture was already forming in her thoughts.

Kay sat up suddenly, her mind reeling with the immensity of what she saw. She broke her concentration, but even when she had recovered she could not still the vision of that brief and awesome moment. An infinity of stars and the boundless sea of the universe.

Who was this girl?

CHAPTER FOUR

THE FOREST WAS A CATHE-
dral of tall pine, dark alder, oak and mountain ash. The tree tops
resounded with the chatter of birds. Wild creatures scampered
through the undergrowth. It was a world of great and small;
pillars of wood rose to the sky while at their feet grew minia-
ture flowers, blue-eyed grass and peeping mushrooms. A soft
light suffused the air as the green dimness of leaves blended
with the earthy brown of the forest floor.

Kay and Aherne had been walking since dawn. The forest
became increasingly dense as they left the high slopes and
moved downward into the valley. They were travelling westwards in search of the twin peaks of Ton Dubh where Fintan
Tuan dwelled.

With quiet concern Kay kept an eye on the younger girl.
In the light of day Aherne seemed even slighter and more frail.
Her face was unnaturally white and pinched from lack of sleep
and nourishment. They had managed to fashion rough coverings for her feet by tearing up the groundsheet but her ragged
clothes were poor protection from the cool damp air. Though
Kay divided the tea and sandwiches remaining in her backpack
it wasn't enough for a long day's tramp. She knew that proper
food and clothing would have to be found before the girl
became seriously ill.

Aherne, however, was more concerned with the threat of wolves and wild boars. She told Kay of fearful nights spent shivering in the high shelter of the trees.

'Don't worry about it,' Kay said with more assurance than she felt. 'They wouldn't attack us in broad daylight.' But she stepped up their pace from that point on.

They forded the River Glancrigh at a shallow bend and rested on its banks before setting out again. They could see the peaks of Ton Dubh in the distance and, though they were footsore and hungry, they were cheered by the sight of their destination. Leaving the forest behind them, they climbed upwards over brushland of gorse and bracken to stony ground and steep slopes of rock.

They talked very little on that long hike. Kay had yet to get used to the novelty of a constant companion and Aherne needed what energy she had to keep herself moving. But they stayed together at all times and helped each other over the roughest parts, both suffering without complaint the sharp pangs of hunger and the ache of tired limbs.

At last they were scaling the high ground of the twin mountains of Ton Dubh, moving cautiously through the craggy gap that lay between.

'There it is!' Kay cried, her voice breaking with strain.

Where the spires of Ton Dubh split like an open mouth, they could see a square shape jutting upwards to the sky. It clung against the precipice like a limpet to a rock, jagged stones haphazardly piled upon each other to form a ruinous but unmistakable tower. Had they not been searching for it, they could easily have overlooked it as part of the mountain. A narrow ledge ran up the cliffside towards the tower.

Aherne let out a moan when she saw the ledge. 'I am afraid of such heights. I cannot go further.' She was trembling and tears began to trickle down her face.

'We must,' Kay insisted, too exhausted to hide her impatience. 'We can't go back now. Hold my hand and don't look down.'

They crept carefully along the ledge, their eyes averted from the sheer drop below. Kay went first, clasping Aherne's hand. Whenever the girl faltered, pressing her face against the rock in a spasm of terror, Kay would grip her all the harder to urge her on. As they neared the tower they discovered with relief that the path steadily widened till they were treading on solid ground once more.

Almost fainting, Aherne leaned on the older girl. Speckles of blood trailed behind her where the sharp stone had pierced the thin coverings on her feet.

'I am sorry for my cowardice,' she whispered, as Kay grasped her around the waist.

'And I'm sorry for being so mean,' Kay said gently. 'Look at your poor feet, and you kept going anyway. You're no coward.'

The tower was before them, less forbidding at closer range and overgrown with brambles of raspberry and ivy. Though it leaned precariously over a deep chasm on one side, the big oaken door was facing directly towards them. And in front of the door was an old man, stooped and moving slowly, pulling at the wild herbs and plants that grew at his feet.

The old man straightened up with a groan and rubbed his back. He wore a rough, dun-coloured tunic and a wide straw hat. A small sack hung over his shoulders, bulging with the berries and greens he had gathered. His face was brown and wrinkled, his eyes cloudy with poor sight, but as soon as he saw the state of the two girls, Kay half-carrying, half-dragging Aherne, he hurried to meet them.

'Are you Fintan Tuan, sir?' Kay asked politely, though her voice was hoarse.

'That is one of my names, daughter,' he replied. 'Welcome to my home. There is rest here for the weary traveller.' He lifted Aherne in his wiry arms and carried her into the tower.

The inside of the tower was even stranger than the outside. As soon as she stepped within, Kay sensed that something was wrong. She followed Fintan through a maze of corridors which meandered endlessly like the secret passageways of the mind. Everything was dark and heavy with silence, and there was an overwhelming feeling of something lost.

They entered a spacious hall shaped like a courtyard but obscured in shadow like the rest of the tower. The floor was strewn with smooth sand. In the centre stood a marble fountain with statues of sea serpents coiling upwards. But no water splashed from the font and the figures were dried and cracked. Kay was looking sadly at these when she noticed the tapestries that covered the high walls, hanging heavily from ceiling to floor. In the dim light of the chamber she could barely discern the outline of intricate pictures lost beneath a film of dust. Her feelings were confirmed. Twilight had settled over this tower and it was but the remains of past grandeur and beauty fled.

Kay did not have long to muse on the state of the hall as Fintan Tuan had carried Aherne past the fountain and through an archway on the far side. She hurried to catch up with them and found herself in a big homely kitchen. The walls were blackened with smoke from the huge hearth which burned a roaring fire. Cupboards and shelves, heaped one upon the other, were filled to overflowing with pots and dishes, jars of pickles and preserves, strongboxes and books. On a top shelf, Kay could see what appeared to be a menagerie of stuffed birds. But when one of them winked at her she realized they were alive and perched comfortably in slumber. From the beams of the roof hung strings of onion and garlic, dried sage and wild peppermint.

The scent of these mingled with the delicious smell of a meaty stew that bubbled in the cauldron over the fire. Kay felt her legs buckle as hunger raged through her.

The old man had set Aherne down in a chair by the hearth to wash and bandage her feet. He murmured gentle words that seemed to revive her. When she sat up and stared around the kitchen she looked much better.

'Right as rain now, eh?' said Fintan with a dry chuckle.

He turned to Kay who was swaying on her feet.

'Sit you down, daughter,' he ordered kindly, pulling another chair to the fire. 'By the Goddess, it must have been a long walk that brought you here.'

Kay slumped into the chair, too weak to talk or move, but the bright flames and the cosy kitchen made her feel warm and safe.

Fintan puttered around them, opening drawers and cupboards, slicing bread, dishing out stew, all the time humming a cheery tune to himself. They didn't eat their meal at the table but sat with their chairs drawn up to the hearth. Cradling the deep wooden bowls in their laps, they dunked the thick gravy with hunks of bread. They ate without speaking, too hungry to stop until they were full, having seconds and thirds and delighting the old man with their appetites. When they were finished he gave them cups of hot cider, and took out a long clay pipe for himself. They sat in happy company, the roaring fire before them, the dark kitchen at their backs, two young girls and the wise old man called Fintan Tuan.

'I have been waiting for both of you,' Fintan said, looking first at one and then the other. Aherne gasped and Kay looked startled but he continued, 'And I see that I have not waited in vain. You have good hearts and your faces show courage and fortitude. You will do well in the task ahead.'

'I think you're mistaken,' Kay began, then she stopped in confusion. A strange sensation was coming over her, the feeling that she knew Fintan somehow and that all was occurring as it should.

The old man gave her an understanding look. 'I am not mistaken.'

His eyes seemed to pierce hers as if he could see not only her thoughts but the trail of her life behind them. 'You have travelled far to meet me, from a place beyond the mountains.'

Kay nodded dumbly.

'And you have come to me for aid, I know. But it is the proper law of life that in order to help yourself you must help others.'

He sat up in his chair. The firelight gleamed in his eyes like twin columns of flame in a dark pool.

'I am Fintan Tuan Mac Cairell, the White Ancient. He who was before recorded time. He who has spun the history of hosts upon his walls. You have seen my hall. The silent fountain. The darkened tapestries. The light has gone from my memory and all that is left is faltering blindness.'

He leaned towards them, his voice low and urgent.

'This darkness is not only mine but that of the race whose history I thread now in this woven world-forgotten place. Twilight is upon us. A time of peril and disorder. The Tuatha De Danaan are approaching their doom.'

Aherne let out a cry but Kay stared at the old man incredulously.

'And there's something *we* can do about it?' she said.

Fintan smiled with wry wisdom.

'That is how it has been since the world began. It is the small and weak who must rise for the good of all. The great are too concerned with their own interests.'

Kay was silent as she considered his words, but it was something he had said earlier that made up her mind. *To help yourself you must help others.* She had already decided to look after Aherne, but it seemed there were more duties to take on before she reached her own goal.

'What do you want us to do?' she said at last.

Fintan took a burning twig from the fire and lit his pipe with long slow puffs.

'You must find the four ancient treasures of the Tuatha De Danaan.'

CHAPTER FIVE

Evening drew on. The hearth fire glowed in a labyrinth of red ashy caves. Wind whistled round the corners of the tower. The two girls sat spellbound as the old man told them a story of the Golden Age of the Tuatha De Danaan.

''Twas in the early days of the world when the tribe of Danu lived in the Hyperborean Lands far beyond the winds of time. Four cities they raised up by art and magic. Bright Gorias of the fiery mountains. Fair Findias of the cold white snow. Sea-shining Murias and Failias, the City of Stone. They shone like jewels on the crown of the earth and all within was splendid and beautiful, harmonious and grand. And in these cities four treasures were made to be a link of power that would exalt the Danaan race.

'In the fires of Gorias, they forged the Sword. Slender as a hazel wand but whistling with two-edged vigour, it had a blade of diamond and an ivory hilt.

'In the icy air of Findias, they shaped the Spear. An upright weapon, it was finely pointed with diamond tip and shaft of ivory.

'In the warm waters of Murias was cast the Cauldron. A round-bellied vessel, beautiful in form like the others, it had a rim of diamond and an ivory bowl.'

Fintan paused and his voice took on a deeper timbre.

'In the finest of cities stood the finest of treasures. In Failias was raised the Lia Fail, the Stone of Destiny that sings truth and fate into the world. All that is right, all that is to be, proceeds from its voice.'

'The Singing Stone!' cried Kay. 'That's what I was looking for myself. But I found it already. It brought me here and then disappeared again.'

Fintan nodded slowly. 'Indeed you found the Stone for it called out to you, but though it chose to carry you here it does not sing in this land. Only when the four treasures are united will their true power shine forth. Then will my hall and memory be rekindled and then each of you shall find what you seek.'

'This is spiralling on and on,' Kay said, dazed.

'Naturally, daughter,' Fintan replied in a gently admonishing tone. 'The spiral is the symbol of life. Nothing runs in straight lines or completed circles. That is false perception.'

'But what became of the cities?' Aherne asked. 'Why do my people no longer dwell in them? And what happened to the treasures?'

Fintan sighed heavily before he answered her.

'The treasures were made of ivory, diamond and stone. But while ivory is pure and stone unchanging, the beauty of diamond conceals a flaw.' He gazed into the fire now cooling into dove-grey ash. 'There was a flaw in the treasures, a flaw in the race of Danu. The link of power that should have exalted your race was not rightly forged. A darkness came over the cities of glory and their end drew near. The Tuatha De Danaan built a great fleet and set sail upon the far-flung seas till they came at last to this sweet isle. They called it Inisfail, Island of Destiny, in honour of the Stone and they burned their ships in the belief that they had found a new home.'

'And the treasures?' prompted Aherne.

'Oh, they came too,' Fintan said dryly. 'Though the linking of the four had failed, the treasures had power of their own and they brought prosperity and grandeur to the Danaans of Inisfail. But with the passing of each generation the memory of the old days grew dimmer. Two treasures were lost, two forgotten, and they are now scattered over the land.'

'So how are we to find them?' Kay asked.

Though he had seemed to gain dignity in the telling of his tale, Fintan now lapsed back into the manner of a doddery old man. He poked the dead fire with a listless foot and fumbled over his pipe.

'That I can't tell you,' he said finally, avoiding their eyes. 'You will have to search blindly. But this I do know. If you seek with your heart, with your instinct for the true, the treasures will find you.'

The girls looked at him with dismay. Both could feel the weariness of the long day dragging them down and neither liked the idea of such a hopeless task.

Fintan slapped his thigh with a sudden burst of joviality.

'It's not as bad as all that. No worse than life itself. You never know what you are looking for until it finds you.' And his laugh was infectious enough to make them smile. Then his face grew gentle. 'I will help you on your way, do not fear. You are both young and you'll feel fit and ready after a good night's sleep.'

He led them out of the kitchen and up a narrow stairway to a little bower. There were thick rugs on the floor and a big goose-feathered bed with woollen blankets. As soon as Fintan left, Aherne jumped on the bed with a cry of delight.

'Far better than a prickly tree or the cold cruel ground!' And she quickly undressed.

Kay laughed as the coloured rags were tossed into the air. 'We'll have to ask him for some clothes for you.'

But Aherne didn't reply. She was already under the covers and well on her way to sleep.

Kay smiled at the girl wryly and began to pace the room. Worrying about Aherne had kept Kay's mind from her own problems, but now in the silence of the tower they crowded around her like dark angels. What was she doing on this adventure? Was there some secret design that she wasn't aware of? With sudden decision, she crept quietly out of the room and down the stairs to Fintan's kitchen.

The hearth was cold but a candle flickered on the wooden table, casting bright shadows through the darkened room. A black shape was hunched in one of the chairs and Kay started with fright as two eyes suddenly opened to stare at her.

'I couldn't sleep,' she said, when she realized it was Fintan.

'I know,' he replied. 'I've been waiting for you.'

He pointed to the chair opposite him. They sat facing each other with the flame of the candle between.

'What do you see when you look at me?' Fintan asked her.

Surprised by the question, Kay stumbled over her words.

'Uh . . . an old man,' she said, then added hastily, 'not meaning to be rude.'

Fintan's face crinkled with humour.

'I can accept truth over courtesy.'

He gave her a long look. 'But what do you see when you *think* of me?'

Kay trembled as a rush of fear passed through her.

'Come, come,' Fintan said firmly. 'You have already used it once by your own choice. It is now yours and under your command.'

Kay's eyes widened. Was he talking about the pictures in her mind? But how could he know? Relief mingled with her fear and there was also a rising excitement that left her breathless. *It was now hers and under her command.*

Rigid in her chair, she stared at the lined face across from her. As she had done with Aherne, Kay concentrated on the man before her. It seemed easier now. The images came in quick and clear succession.

A great hawk beat its wings against the sky, a noble creature with eyes that burned like coals. Now a salmon, sleek and silvery, lying in a deep pool shaded by trees. Finally a man, tall as a king, with ancient wisdom shining in his features.

The images faded and, without thinking, Kay bowed her head towards Fintan. It was an old man who sat before her but she sensed also another presence, one of immense power and knowledge.

'I am Tuan,' he said. 'I am the hawk of time and the salmon of wisdom. I am the *Ruad Ro-fhessa,* the Lord of Surpassing Knowledge.'

'And what am I?' Kay asked him.

Fintan smiled at her gently but his eyes were veiled.

'You are that which you are becoming. I cannot name it because you have not yet become it.' He shook his head apologetically. 'That's the trouble with time. I don't live within it, and I know you in the future as well as the past and the now. I can't answer your question as it doesn't fit here. But you will know soon enough and then we shall talk again, I promise.'

Kay understood that their conversation was over and she could see Fintan's eyes closing with sleep. As she stood up from the table, he added a final comment.

'You have accepted the power of your mind. It is a rare gift and it can go further. Do not be afraid to use it.'

'Thank you,' Kay murmured, but Fintan's head was already nodding on his chest. His breath came in slow whistles like the wind.

⋆   ⋆   ⋆

The next morning Kay and Aherne found themselves abandoned in the tower. Hall and corridor were silent and empty. Fintan Tuan could not be found.

'Has he deserted us?' Aherne asked anxiously.

In the kitchen, they found a meal left out for them on the table, thick slices of bread dripping with honey and bowls of frothy milk. And beside the food was a bright heap of clothing.

'They're definitely for us,' Kay said happily as she sorted through the pile.

There were two of everything in a size to fit each girl; trousers of supple brown hide, long-sleeved blouses of white wool, and leather sandals that laced up to the knee. Best of all were the broad cloaks of forest-green with deep cowls that would keep out rain and wind.

'Beautiful!' Aherne said. She twirled the mantle around her and fastened its golden brooch. 'I love the colour green.'

Kay was inspecting the border that trimmed the cloak from hood to hem. Lost in thought she traced the threaded symbol with her finger. A gold-stitched pattern of triple spirals.

'They are ideal clothes for travelling,' Aherne said, aware of Kay's silence.

'Yes,' Kay said absently, 'he said he would help us on our way.' She looked closely at Aherne. There was a flush of colour in the girl's thin face and a healthier light in her eyes. Fintan's hearty food and the long night's sleep had done her a lot of good. 'You look much better. Are you up for a journey?'

Aherne nodded eagerly and Kay laughed.

'Well then, all we have to do is figure out where we're going.'

As they ate their breakfast, the two discussed the task that Fintan had given them.

'It's a quest,' Kay said. 'Just like the stories in my books. Except we have four things to find instead of the usual one.'

'The four ancient treasures of my race,' Aherne said. Her voice echoed with awe. 'The Sword, the Spear, the Cauldron and the Stone.'

'But where to start looking for them?' said Kay. 'I wish Fintan hadn't disappeared like that. The least he could've done was left us a hint or a sign or something.'

She remembered the stormy night in Bray and the message sent to her from the sea. A triple spiral, the same pattern as the one on her cloak.

'Does this mean anything to you?' she asked Aherne, pointing to the spirals.

'It is the symbol of Danu,' Aherne said with a shrug, as if stating the obvious. 'The three eyes of the Goddess.'

'I don't see how that can help,' Kay muttered with disappointment.

They were quiet a while and then Aherne's face lit up.

'It is the sign! So clear and simple, I almost missed it!' Her voice rose with excitement. 'The symbol of Danu is set in stone upon a sacred place. The Brugh na Boinne. The White Mound on the banks of the River Boann. They say it holds untold wealth and treasure.'

Kay slapped the table. 'We're on the road. That must be where we should go.'

But now Aherne looked anxious. 'It is a forbidden place where only the Druids go. Death is its promise to any intruder.'

Kay caught Aherne's fear and shivered despite her cloak. With a deliberate effort she shrugged off the warning.

'Let's not worry about that till we get there.'

Kay didn't express the thought that had suddenly struck her. They had no idea what kind of dangers they would face on this quest.

CHAPTER SIX

Ⓜ AG BREGA WAS THE
broad rolling plain that lay between the great rivers of the
Rurthach and the Boann. The girls had to march through
the mountains to reach it, tramping by day across peak and
valley and sleeping by night in the hollows of trees. The
journey was long and the way arduous, but the rich air of
the highlands brought colour to their faces and strength to
their limbs. They had parcels of food from Fintan's larder as
well as the wild plants and berries foraged from the woods.
Though they argued now and then about the route they
would take, both grew accustomed to each other's company
on those long days and nights. By the time they forded the
rushing waters of the Rurthach, leaving the mountains
behind them and facing the plain, they were already moving
as a team.

Their second night on Mag Brega, they sat in front of the
camp fire, tired but pleased with their progress. At this pace they
would reach the River Boann and the Brugh na Boinne by the
following day. Their cloaks were wrapped tightly around them
against the wind that came whistling over the grasslands. Above
shone the pale shell of the moon, free of cloud and dispelling
cool light into the sky. Around them spread the landscape in
dark relief, a vast silhouette of lilting plain and low hill.

Whatever made the girls look in the same direction at the same time could not be named. Each was instantly overcome with the feeling that they were being watched, as if a thousand eyes in the night had suddenly trained on them. Both gasped at what they saw, Kay in awe, Aherne with unbridled horror.

There upon a distant hill top three riders appeared against the moonlit sky. They rode upon gigantic stags with antlers like the branches of some mighty tree. The riders too were giants and antlered also, the jagged shapes rising from their brows like magnificent crowns. Hair and cloaks streamed in the wind as they came to a halt on the summit of the hill. Then they dispersed—one to the north, one to the south and one to the west.

The sighting had taken but a moment and yet Kay felt as if her mind had been scorched by a raging fire. Whoever the riders were they had left the stamp of their existence in the deepest part of her thoughts. Here was something beyond humankind, something incredibly old and wild, not of man and not of beast. Elemental creatures of the uncharted night. For the first time since she had arrived in Inisfail, Kay felt truly afraid.

Aherne slumped forward, burying her face in her hands.

'Who were they? What were they?' Kay demanded, shaken.

'They are the Sentinels,' Aherne whispered. When she looked at Kay her green eyes were dark with despair. 'The three Sentinels of the Tuatha De Danaan. Fiac, Rusc and Radarc. They are not of our people but are children of the Goddess, birthed from the womb of the earth. They ride at the command of the Druids but they are beyond Danaan law. The time is forgotten when they were last called into the land. Something terrible has happened.'

'Why?' said Kay, trying to regain her calm. 'Why are they called? What do they do?'

'For one purpose do they ride.' Aherne let out a moan. 'Their duty is to kill.'

She stared into the fire and her voice quavered.

'Our most sacred law tells us that Danaan cannot kill Danaan. The Sentinels are called when one of our own must die. Someone has committed a dreadful deed. Some noble Danaan is condemned to die. Darkness and disorder have entered the land.' She started to weep. 'I feel as I did before you came to me, Kay. All is falling apart. All is lost and hopeless.'

'Pull yourself together,' Kay said, half-pleading, half-commanding. 'Don't collapse on me now.'

'But what can we do?' Aherne wailed. 'Murder has entered the land!' Her sobs grew louder.

'Stop it!' Kay shouted.

Kay herself was very close to the same state as Aherne. Their plight was undeniable. They were alone in a dark countryside and helpless against attack. The sight of the Sentinels had brought that home with terrifying clarity. But Kay was determined to keep her fear under control—and Aherne's as well.

The younger girl was looking at her with dismay, shocked out of her weeping by Kay's angry tone.

'They're gone now and we're all right,' Kay said firmly. 'Hysterics won't help us any.'

Aherne sniffed quietly to herself as she slowly recovered.

'It is not fair,' she mumbled. 'Fintan did not warn us of danger.'

'That's a thought,' Kay said with sudden encouragement. 'He sent us out into this land with a job to do. Obviously he believes we can handle it whether it's dangerous or not.'

Aherne grew calmer as she considered this. She touched the pattern on the hem of her cloak, letting her fingers run over the golden spirals.

'And we agreed to take on the quest,' Kay pointed out, 'so we could find the answers to our own questions. It's not as if we're doing this just for Fintan.'

'Yes,' Aherne said, gathering her strength. 'This quest is for my own cause. If there is danger in finding out who I am, then I must be prepared to face it.'

'So whatever happens,' Kay went on, 'whatever we discover or suffer or learn . . .'

'We must follow the quest,' Aherne finished.

They stared at each other in silence as courage and determination rose in each.

'Tomorrow the Brugh,' Aherne said softly.

'Let's get some sleep,' Kay said with a nod.

Calmed by their own resolve, the girls lay down to sleep, pulling their cloaks over them like blankets.

'Kay?' said Aherne after a while.

'Hmm?'

'Were you very angry when you shouted at me?'

'Not really,' Kay answered, looking up at the sky. 'To be honest, I was frightened. Not just because of the Sentinels but by you as well. I'm used to being on my own. I don't know what to do when you get like that. I just can't handle it. I guess I need you to be strong as well.'

'Then I shall try to be strong,' Aherne promised fervently.

'Go to sleep,' said Kay, but she smiled to herself as she closed her eyes.

They were up early the next day to complete their march across the plain. Before them lay the river valley of the Boann. The fertile lands that bordered the river rolled higher than Mag Brega. Field after field rustled with the golden wealth of oats and barley, wheat and rye. It was the first sign of civilization the girls had encountered in their travels and they crept through the hills, avoiding settlements and field-workers alike.

When they reached the River Boann, they travelled along its banks accompanied by the melodious sound of the dark rushing waters. By midday they crossed the ford of Ros na Righ and hurried eastward towards their goal. They moved furtively at all times, uneasy in the daylight. They were heading for a forbidden place and they didn't want anyone to see or question them.

When they came at last to the Brugh na Boinne, they stared up at it with anxious awe.

It was a massive cairn of stone, smooth and white, standing on a hill that overlooked the river. Like a half-moon, rounded in shape, its surface was a coat of glistening quartz. It seemed cold and ominous, glaring white in the sunshine, like a sepulchre masking its dark contents.

And surrounding the mound was a circle of giant standing stones. Dark guards before the pale face of the Brugh. Their message was clear. *Do not enter here.*

'Maybe we should wait till night-time,' Kay said. 'Then we'll have some cover.'

Aherne disagreed fearfully.

'It is at night that the Druids use the heavy chambers of darkness. If we must go in, we should do it now.'

'Well, let's hope our cloaks camouflage us,' Kay said, pulling up her hood. 'I'm sure you can see this place for miles around.'

They crawled carefully up the hillside towards the White Mound, thankful for the cover of the tall meadow grass. As they neared the ring of standing stones, Kay reached out suddenly to hold Aherne back.

'There's something there,' she whispered. 'Can you feel it?'

Aherne shook her head with a puzzled look. Kay stared suspiciously at the stones. Each stood separately, grey and stolid, in threatening pose. There was plenty of space for the girls to pass through, but Kay's mind was tingling strangely, as if a tiny alarm had been set off.

'Can we avoid them?' she asked Aherne.

'They make a full circle,' came the low reply.

'Then, we'll have to go through,' Kay muttered though her instincts warred against her.

Still low to the ground, they crept towards the stones. They had no sooner entered the shadow of the circle when they found they couldn't move. Like insects caught in a spider's web, they were bound fast by invisible threads. Worse sensations followed. A current of energy began to course through them, sapping their strength.

Aherne panicked and her cry came out like a strangled sob. Kay's reaction was one of helpless fury.

'I knew it!' she swore to herself. 'I knew it was a trap. Why didn't I listen to my mind?'

She could feel the unseen force draining her will like a predator feeding on blood and she knew that it meant to kill her. Her anger grew. She didn't want to die. Not when there was still so much to know.

'Stop it!' she thought furiously. 'I won't let you kill me!'

At that very moment Kay sensed the force weaken a little as if retreating in response to her thought.

Can I fight you? she wondered

She felt strangely calm despite the danger and she marvelled at her own strength. But didn't Fintan tell her she had power? Buoyed by this thought, she began her efforts in earnest. The battle was on.

Like a young warrior testing her skills, Kay bent her mind to fight the enemy. Her confidence grew as she sensed the weakness of her adversary. This was mindless force laid on the stones by Druidic chant. Effective and undoubtedly fatal to the powerless intruder, it had no defence against a counter attack. Still it wasn't easy. Each stone reinforced the other with its silent deadly commands and Kay found herself wrestling them one by one. Though her mind strained with the intensity of the struggle and she wondered at times if she could keep it up, Kay began to sense that she was winning. The web was loosening its hold. Slowly at first and then with more ease, Kay was able to move. She reached out painfully to grasp Aherne. With a final burst of effort, she broke through the circle, dragging herself and Aherne beyond the shadow of the stones.

But the battle had taken its toll. Kay collapsed on the ground, her mind numb with pain.

Freed from the circle, Aherne soon revived and she leaned over Kay with concern and astonishment.

'You saved us!' she said. 'Are you ill? What can I do?'

'Help me up for starters,' Kay said weakly, but her voice was triumphant as Aherne lifted her to her feet. 'I'll recover, don't worry. I've got a splitting headache but the rest of me seems fine.'

'How did you . . . ?' Aherne was looking at Kay with new respect.

Kay shrugged with embarrassment. 'It's all new to me. I seem to have some kind of mind power.'

'Then we are not as defenceless in this quest as we thought,' Aherne said, smiling proudly at her companion.

'I guess not,' Kay said with a grin. 'Shall we continue?'

They approached the mound cautiously. The entrance was a dark mouth blocked by a huge lintel stone scored with designs. Kay stared at the triple spirals that whorled like eyes and eyes.

'Right on track,' she said with a satisfied grimace. 'I hope there are no more booby traps.'

They had to climb over the lintel stone to enter the Brugh. After a moment's hesitation, fearing more powerful curses, they did so. The mound opened before them and they moved uneasily into a long dim tunnel. Great stones ranged on either side. They were forced to walk in single file, Kay stooping at times where the roof was too low for her height. They could sense the massive weight above them, tons of stone heaped over this slender passageway. The air was cold and stale like a tomb. They walked heavily, aware at every step that they were treading on forbidden ground.

The dimness lifted suddenly as the tunnel widened into a chamber with a high dome of corbelled rock.

'The heart's core,' Aherne whispered.

Three alcoves faced them, hewn in the walls of the rock like a great cloverleaf. The two alcoves on the right and left cast out a multicoloured light and the girls caught their breath when they saw why. Each recess held a dazzling hoard of treasure.

The riches spilled over ledges and rose in bright heaps. Gems winked like the eyes of a peacock. Tiaras and diadems shone like crystal. Sun-discs glittered like plates of gold. There were silver basins inlaid with red and purple stones, vessels and dishes of copper and bronze. Gold glimmered in all its hues, honey-yellow, dark orange and white, fashioned into fabulous jewellery and ornaments. Bracelets and gorgets, brooches and earrings, necklaces and breast-pins all lay tangled together in sparkling piles. And leaning upright like opulent warriors were weapons of the finest metal: long sharp swords and spears tall as men; great shields embossed with knobs of gold; and enamelled scabbards red as blood.

Kay stared curiously at the copious wealth. 'I don't see *our* treasures,' she muttered to herself, then turned to the alcove directly in front of her. It was dark and seemingly empty of treasure. The floor was covered with a mat of branches that had been stripped bare and skilfully intertwined. On the mat was a smooth stone engraved with triskelion designs. Hanging over the stone, like a heavy canopy, was a thick hide that gave off an acrid scent. The stern simplicity of the cell and the wordless meaning of its objects struck Kay immediately.

'There is something here,' she said.

Aherne nodded and pointed to the mat. 'The wattles of wisdom upon which the Druids lie. And they place the stone upon their chest while the bull hide above brings the darkness of visions.' She shivered as the symbols of the Druidic priesthood reminded her that she was profaning a sacred place.

Kay had already stepped into the alcove and was touching the bull hide reverently. Her face looked dark and unhappy.

'My mind is still weak. I'm getting images but they're very dim. Yes! I see it now! A sword. It must be our Sword!' Her excitement was rising but there was disappointment as well. 'It's not here. It's in another place.' She shook her head. 'I can't recognize . . .'

'Describe it to me,' Aherne urged.

'I see a mountain overlooking a bay. There's a huge stone wall on top of the mountain. Round like a bowl. And a sort of castle inside.'

'Grianan Ailech!' Aherne cried. 'Our fortress in the north!'

Kay let go of the bull hide as the images faded.

'That's where the Sword is,' she said to Aherne. 'Now we know the first treasure to find and where—'

She froze suddenly even as Aherne's face went white. The sound they least expected but secretly dreaded came to them. Footsteps in the tunnel.

CHAPTER SEVEN

As THE FOOTSTEPS DREW
near, the girls looked at each other in panic. Escape was impossible. Kay pulled Aherne into the alcove and down behind the canopy. Crouched in the shadows of the bull hide, behind the Druidic stone, they could still see into the chamber. Their hearts beat wildly as three men entered.

The men were tall and elderly, dressed in dark blood-coloured robes and black tasselled mantles that swept the floor. Around their necks shone collars of beaten gold which arched high behind their ears and curved down over their breasts. Their hair and beards were grey-white with age. They walked with an air of eminence and authority. But while one man's face was kind, the other two looked haughty, even cruel.

Kay felt their power pressing down on her mind and she stilled her own thoughts in case they might sense her. She guessed they were Druids but it was Aherne who recognized them with dread. The three Chief Druids of Inisfail—Fiss and Fokmar, the Dark Ones, with Eolas, the Wise.

Fiss and Fokmar talked quietly together. Their whispers rasped through the chamber like metal striking stone. Eolas waited patiently, barely concealing his contempt. It was Fokmar who finally addressed him.

'We are happy that you agreed to this secret council, Eolas. There is much to be discussed.'

'I join you for one reason only,' Eolas replied. His voice was deep and calm but it rang with command. 'Who called up the Sentinels? And who is their prey?'

Looks were passed between the two dark Druids.

'We called the Sentinels,' said Fiss. 'We did not inform you, knowing that you would oppose us. As for their prey,' he hesitated a moment and then spat out the answer, 'they ride to kill Eriu.'

Eolas's face contorted with shock even as Kay felt Aherne stiffen beside her.

'Have you gone mad?' Eolas cried. 'You would kill the Rising Queen? The rage of the Goddess will fall upon us!'

'The rage of the Goddess falls upon all traitors,' Fokmar said harshly. Then he raised his hand as if to bring peace to the council. His voice took on a smooth, insinuating tone. 'Only a few days ago, Eolas, it was you who warned us of an approaching invasion of our land.'

Still reeling with what he had heard, Eolas spoke in a dazed voice.

'I do not deny the visions of the bull-sleep. The *tairfeis* is truth. I have seen a fawn pursued by a red-eared hound. In the sky, winged serpents raged in battle. And when the Lady rode her pale horse, she was overcome by a rider upon his black steed. Since the beginning of time these have been the omens of conquest.'

'We too have lain upon the wattles of wisdom,' Fiss said softly, 'and the bull-sleep has shown us more. Fokmar it was who saw the land emptied of our people. And I myself saw the reason why.'

A hush fell over the chamber. Kay and Aherne held their breaths, afraid that the slightest sound would be heard.

Fiss's voice rose with strident malice.

'I saw Eriu embrace the enemy king in her arms.'

Eolas's face went white. He stared with disbelief at his fellow Druid. But no priest could lie about the revelations of the *tairfeis*.

Fiss continued. 'That is why our visions foretell doom and conquest. The Tuatha De Danaan have never known defeat but there is no doubt that we could be undone by treachery. The weak link that would destroy us is our next queen.'

'If she dies before she rises to power,' Fokmar added, 'that link will be broken. The hill forts are armed and we have sent heralds to call the warriors to their hostings. We will be ready when our shores are invaded and the death of Eriu will ensure our victory.'

Eolas swayed on his feet as if their words were sharp knives piercing his heart, but still he struggled against them.

'It is the seventh year. Danaan law demands a change of sovereignty. Banba and Fodla have already ruled. If their sister is not to rise, who then will be queen in Inisfail?'

Fiss and Fokmar exchanged glances. It was obvious that they had prepared their answers.

Fokmar smiled thinly. 'Sovereignty is but a symbol and that symbol is the royal sword. Any noble Danaan woman is fit to represent the Goddess in this land. At the games of Tailltiu on the feast of Lugnasad we will present the sword to the winner of the women's race. With sovereignty assured and our armies ready, the Tuatha De Danaan will meet the enemy full-strong and invincible.'

Eolas closed his eyes. When he opened them again, they were dark with bitterness.

'You have laid your plans well and I am not surprised. You have plotted against Eriu since her early youth. She has shown more promise than any ruler we have had for generations. You have always feared that her rise to power would put an end to yours.'

Fiss reddened at these words but Fokmar shrugged coldly.

'There is no need for insults, Eolas. It is only natural that you would favour Eriu's succession as she is your foster-child. But you must put aside personal feelings and preferences, no matter how difficult that may be. Our past quarrels are now irrelevant. We face the threat of conquest. Hard decisions must be made. Do you accept that Fiss has told you the truth about his vision?'

It was some time before Eolas could bring himself to answer. Though he knew the two Druids schemed always for power, they would never, could never, lie about the *tairfeis*. It was the foundation of Druidic belief, the cornerstone of power, the sacred bond with the Goddess. A priest would lose his life if he desecrated its name.

When Eolas finally bowed his head in assent, the weight of grief seemed to pull him downwards. He stood a stooped and broken man.

With quiet triumph, Fokmar dealt the last blow.

'Then you accept that Eriu is traitor. The law cannot be denied its honour-price. Death is the penalty for treason.'

'My poor, poor dear,' Eolas murmured. His face was wet with tears. He did not look again at Fiss and Fokmar. With an air of defeat and utter loss, he left the chamber in silence, dragging his feet like a man condemned.

When he was gone, the two Druids smiled at each other with undisguised glee.

'The old fool,' hissed Fokmar. 'But at least he knows when he is beaten. It would not bode well if the Chief Druids were divided in their counsel to the people. Now our plans can proceed without interference. What have your spies reported? Are there any signs of an enemy fleet?'

Fiss did not have time to answer for at that very moment a slight but unmistakable sound echoed through the chamber. The two Druids were suddenly silent and alert.

Behind the canopy Kay and Aherne went rigid with fright. Both had been listening intently to the council. Kay had perked up at the mention of the royal sword and was wondering if it was the same sword she was seeking. But it was the talk of the queen's death and the coming invasion that had affected Aherne. These were terrible tragedies befalling her tribe and she couldn't stop the tears from welling up to blind her. Without thinking, she had lifted her arm to wipe her eyes. In that second of carelessness, the brooch which clasped her cloak struck against the Druidic stone.

Fokmar's eyes darted throughout the chamber and settled on the sacred alcove. As his glance penetrated the shadows of the bull hide, his eyes flashed with anger.

'There!' he cried. 'Intruders!'

As soon as Fokmar shouted, the girls were up and running. They had no time to plan or confer, but the teamwork of their travels helped them act with one mind. Arms linked and heads down like a battering ram, they charged forward. Speed and surprise were on their side as they barrelled through the Druids to race down the tunnel.

It was a brief but terrifying run. At last the entranceway opened before them. Daylight blinded their eyes as they leaped over the lintel stone.

'The circle!' Kay gasped with a sinking heart.

Beyond stood the ring of massive stones waiting pitilessly to ensnare them.

Kay quailed at the thought of another battle. It was too soon, she was certain. Her mind wasn't strong enough. But what else could they do? The Druids had recovered. Footsteps rang behind them.

'Never give up!' she cried, catching Aherne's hand as they ran towards the stones.

It was hopeless and yet they ran with hope in their hearts. Fear raged through them and yet they insisted on being courageous. They neared the circle, steeling themselves for the onslaught of power. But though they were ready to face the worst, they were not prepared for what did happen.

They heard a voice, high up in the air, deep and unearthly but strangely compelling. They stopped, unsure and disoriented. Then the air itself parted before them as if a curtain had been torn asunder. There beyond all imagining stood a giant of a man with antlered brow and a cloak of green leaves. His face was sharp and wild like a blue-eyed hawk's. His yellow hair fell back from his forehead like a horse's mane. Beside him was a magnificent stag with shining hide and antlers of awesome width. Together they were an image of impossible beauty.

The man spoke again in his rich and vibrant voice.

'Enter, brave children, into the *feth fiada,* the god-hedge of a Sentinel.'

They were not given a choice nor the chance to resist. The air simply closed around them, enveloping them in a secret space, milky white and soundless. The world outside was but a shadow.

CHAPTER EIGHT

Out of the frying pan and into the fire, Kay was thinking to herself.

The Sentinel had grasped hold of the girls and was leading them through the milky void. Though they could barely see, they were aware of each other and the giant man with his companion beast. At one point they stopped abruptly as footsteps sounded just beyond them. They knew someone was near but it was like looking at a shadow at the bottom of a murky pool. The figure stopped. Two eyes glowed like points of fire to pierce the veil of invisibility. The girls knew they were seen but whoever it was simply turned and left them.

'Eolas,' said Aherne with a sigh of relief. 'The Druids are not deceived by magic, but he let us be.'

'The others won't,' Kay muttered.

As if he heard her words, the Sentinel moved beside them and again the air was torn away. They were on the hillside below the Brugh. The circle of stones stood a safe distance behind. Fiss and Fokmar were at the entrance of the mound, pointing in their direction and shouting for guards.

The Sentinel acted swiftly. He lifted the girls onto the stag's broad back and in a flash was up behind them. His great arms encircled Kay and Aherne as the stag made a breathtaking leap into the air. With dizzying speed they bounded for the river to hurtle over the water as if they were flying. The ground rose to meet them on the other side. Though the girls were winded by the sharp drop, the stag charged onwards without breaking his stride.

Westwards they rode, leaving the Brugh na Boinne behind them.

It was a wondrous ride. The very existence of such a creature inspired awe in the girls. And they were aware also of the giant that rode along with them, half-man, half-god, son of the Mother Earth. Though they had no idea why he had rescued them or what he intended to do, their anxiety was lulled by the graceful motion of the stag and the hush of the countryside that blurred around them.

Whether from shock at their close escape or the long days of travelling, the girls eventually dozed into sleep, cradled from a fall by the Sentinel's arms. When the stag came to a halt in a leafy wood, they found themselves being lifted down.

'Now little ones,' said the Sentinel, 'we shall rest and eat.'

They stared at him warily, not knowing what he would do if they tried to escape. But he seemed oblivious to their concern as he set about building the fire and preparing their meal. He took a leather satchel from beneath his cloak and arranged food and utensils with skilful care. Dried beef, wild apples and fat mushrooms were all speared on skewers and roasted over the flames. Though the girls were hesitant to draw near, they couldn't resist the smells that came wafting their way. They sat down by the fire and took the food he offered them, all the time keeping a close watch on his actions.

He moved with the elegant grace of one who has always lived in the open. His cloak of green leaves rustled like the trees. His antlers arched like branches. Beneath his cloak he wore red-brown hide. A great stone dagger hung at his waist.

Like the stag he rode, he was untamed and free, a creature of the forests and the windy plains. When he sat to eat with them, his eyes stared over the fire as keen and as remote as a hawk's.

Kay cleared her throat as she found the courage to speak. Her tone was respectful.

'May I ask why you rescued us from the Druids? Don't they command you?'

The Sentinel bowed his head towards Kay. She felt a twinge of shock when she saw where the antlers jutted from his brow. She had only begun to grasp that he wasn't human.

'I am Radarc, Sentinel of Danu,' he said in a deep tranquil voice. 'I serve all who belong to my Mother, the Goddess. You wear Her symbol on your cloak, I saw it shining as you ran. Those who pursued you intended your death and I knew this should not be. All else concerns me not.'

'You mean you don't care who we are or what we're doing?' Kay said, surprised.

'I and my brothers have been called into the land for one purpose,' Radarc replied, and he repeated, 'all else concerns me not.'

'Then we are free to go!' Aherne burst out, not bothering to hide her relief. 'We are not your prisoners!'

Kay thought she saw a flicker of pain in the Sentinel's eyes but it was difficult to tell.

'I took you from danger,' he said quietly. 'I did not think it was against your will. I would hold no living creature in bondage.'

They followed his glance to where the stag grazed freely without saddle or tether.

'We appreciate your help, believe me,' Kay said hastily. 'It's just that we know . . . well, what you do . . . I mean, that made us think you'd be dangerous.'

The Sentinel's face was impassive.

'I am,' he said, 'but only to my prey.'

Aherne's face darkened. Her emotions rose in her voice.

'You are riding to kill the Rising Queen. How can you bring such evil to Inisfail?'

'I do not bring evil,' Radarc said evenly. 'I ride to meet it. The law and the judgement are of your people. I am but the executioner.'

'It is an evil deed nonetheless,' Aherne said. Her voice echoed the sorrow and confusion of Eolas.

'Where are you riding to now?' Kay asked the Sentinel.

She was hoping to change the subject as it was upsetting Aherne, but she realized her error as soon as Radarc answered.

'I am riding to Grianan Ailech. Eriu has fled her palace and I believe she may have sought refuge in that northernmost citadel. I hope to end my hunt there.'

Aherne burst into tears at the bluntness of Radarc's intent but Kay's heart jumped at the mention of Grianan Ailech. She saw the opportunity before her and felt compelled to take it, despite Aherne's feelings.

'That's where we want to go too!' she said eagerly. 'Will you take us with you?'

'I will not ride with a murderer!' Aherne cried before the Sentinel could reply. Her face was streaked with tears and her look was wild.

'You didn't object when he saved us,' Kay retorted impatiently.

But she was unnerved by the storm of Aherne's emotions. The girl was impossible to reason with in such a state.

'I will not ride with him,' Aherne repeated stubbornly.

Kay's anger rose as she considered the consequences of Aherne's refusal. Without thinking she leaned forward to grab Aherne by her cloak.

'If you think I'm walking all the way just because of you . . .'

Aherne drew back, startled by Kay's threatening pose, then she burst into tears again.

Kay was exasperated but her voice grew calmer.

'You promised me you'd be strong. Remember? And we're supposed to follow the quest no matter what happens. You agreed to that too. The Sword is in Grianan Ailech. We must go there and it'll be a lot faster and easier if he takes us.'

Aherne nodded in surrender at last. Kay breathed a sigh of relief and turned to Radarc with an apologetic look.

'Can we go with you?' she asked again.

'You may ride with me,' he said. 'We will stay here tonight and leave at dawn.'

Kay thought she heard a note of understanding in his tone, but she wasn't sure. He was too alien to know or understand.

Radarc stoked the fire higher, then left their campsite to walk with his stag in the forest.

Aherne ignored Kay and lay down to sleep, pulling her cloak over her in an angry lonely way. Kay shrugged with annoyance. The girl was a handful at times. And yet, Kay could understand her feelings. Inisfail was Aherne's homeland and her queen was condemned to die. Though Kay could afford to be unaffected by such things, it only made sense that Aherne would take them personally.

'I don't like what he's planning to do either.' She spoke quietly to Aherne's huddled form. 'But maybe the quest will make things better. Fintan said it's for the good of your race.' She saw Aherne's back ease a little and added, 'We have to keep going with hope in our hearts.'

As Kay lay down by the fire, Aherne turned around and reached out silently to take her hand. Kay squeezed the small palm, happy to be friends again.

Later that night, Kay wakened to see two figures beyond the camp fire. It was Radarc standing with his back to the flames, his arm resting on the neck of his stag. Both gazed upwards at the starry night. Deep in her mind Kay could sense the timeless bond between the two. But there was something else as well: a mutual sadness, a shared yearning. For freedom.

Half-awake, Kay was confused. 'Aren't you already free?' But she slipped back into oblivion without an answer to her question.

They rode out the next morning in the early dawn, when the darkness of night still lingered in blue trails over the landscape. The stag bounded northward with the speed and ease of a powerful engine. As the hours passed, the warmth of the rising sun burned away the mists of morning and the countryside shone with brightness and colour. Bronze bog, green hollow, dark plain and white river all swept past in a multihued rush. The journey took a full day, as they stopped for meals. Though Kay expressed concern that the stag was carrying three, the great creature showed no sign of strain or weariness.

By the time they reached Mag Iotha, the plain that bordered the River Fionn, the last bars of sunset were fading from the sky. Twilight descended as they travelled by the River Moghurn and the waters flowed like liquid shadow. At a quiet word from Radarc, the stag left the river to journey westward. Mountains rose before them. They stopped at the peak that held Grianan Ailech like a crown at its summit. Radarc dismounted and lifted the girls down, then spoke gently to his steed.

'Well done, dear friend. We have travelled far with added company. Rest you now till I return.'

The love in his voice affected both Kay and Aherne, for up to then he had seemed so removed from human feeling. Shyly they watched as the Sentinel kissed the stag's forehead before it bounded away.

They were at the foot of the mountain. Above them were the dim stone walls of Grianan Ailech. Danaan cashel of the north, it was a great stone fort overlooking the mountains and the wide bay of Loch Swiligh that emptied into the sea.

'We will enter in secret,' Radarc said, taking the girls by the hand.

Once again they were enfolded in the Sentinel's invisible cloak as he led them up the mountainside. They were uncomfortable walking without sight or sound but the grip of Radarc's hand was reassuring. After a long climb they grew aware of the rise of the walls before them and they stopped even as Radarc did. They waited for some time, not knowing what they were waiting for, till they heard the sound of a gate opening and the stamp of horses riding forth. Radarc lurched forward. The girls scrambled to keep up with him as they entered the fortress.

When the eerie veil was torn away they found themselves in the shadow of the walls. Behind them was a huge oaken gate on bronze hinges. High on the ramparts they could see the outline of warriors keeping watch on the mountains. Before them was the citadel, a vast stone structure of buttressed keeps, hewn stairways, storerooms and halls. The many levels of windows were dark and silent as the cashel slept, except for a single tower that glowed with candlelight.

'Someone resides in the royal chambers,' Radarc said softly. 'If my prey is there, I must take her unawares.'

Aherne let go of the Sentinel's hand with dismay but Kay whispered urgently in her ear. 'We've got to stay with him. There are too many guards!'

While the girls argued in low whispers, Radarc stepped away from them and disappeared. Kay moved quickly to where he had been standing and found the gap that led into a passage inside the fortress wall. She reached out for Aherne to pull her inside before the girl could refuse.

It was pitch dark within. They had to stoop as they walked while the Sentinel was forced to crawl on his hands and knees. But eventually the tunnel grew larger and Radarc was able to stand upright. They climbed stone steps, making their way through the darkness with arms outstretched.

'Hollow walls around the castle?' Kay murmured to Aherne.

'In times of danger,' the girl whispered, 'the people take refuge in here.'

The Sentinel stopped in front of them to push against the wall. With a heavy sigh, the block of stone suddenly gave way. A flood of light blinded the girls and they drew up their hoods to shade their eyes.

Before them was a lovely scene: a royal bower with bright friezes on the walls and rich carpets underfoot. There were lavish couches of embroidered cloth and tall candles in holders studded with gems. But it was not the splendid trappings of the room that caught their eye but the stately lady who sat by the hearth, staring sadly at the flames. She wore a purple gown trimmed with fur. The firelight shone on her yellow-pale hair and the circlet of gold that bound her brow. Though her face was young, there was a weariness in the way she held herself and her eyes were dark with tragedy. Lost in thought, she did not react immediately to the movement of the stone. But when Radarc stepped into her chamber, she sat up startled like a cornered creature. Terror flared in her eyes as she stared at the Sentinel, then she folded her hands and held her head erect.

Seeing the lady's courage, Kay found herself praying hopelessly.

Please, don't be Eriu.

Chapter Nine

To Kay's relief, Radarc approached the lady and bent down on one knee.

'Greetings, Banba, Queen of Inisfail.'

The Queen glanced briefly at the opening in her wall. Her smile was wry.

'The wisdom of the Goddess is yours, Sentinel. Not even I knew of that door.'

'I must know each and every part of the land,' Radarc replied as he stood up again.

'That is understandable,' Banba said, her eyes clouding. 'How else could you carry out your terrible duty?' She sat rigid as if bracing herself for what was to come but her voice was steady. 'Am I your prey?'

'Not you, my Queen,' he answered with surprising gentleness. Then more gently still, 'It is your sister Eriu whom I hunt.'

The Queen lost her composure as her features contorted with disbelief. The sadness of her eyes was magnified to open grief and horror. She cried out.

'Better it were I than she! My time is finished. Eriu is the Rising Queen. What madness is this? She is my rightful successor. Who brings this chaos upon us?'

'It is the will of the Chief Druids,' Radarc said. 'Their visions have named Eriu a traitor to her tribe.'

'I do not believe it! My beloved sister.' Banba wrung her slender hands. 'There is a growing evil in the land and this is but a part of it. I have sensed the storm cloud gathering.'

'Is Eriu with you?' Radarc probed quietly.

'No!' the Queen said with sudden temper. 'And even if she were . . .'

'I uphold the law and so must you,' the Sentinel said evenly, 'I cannot help but think that Eriu is here. Else why are *you* here and not in your palace at Temair?'

The Queen's face was lined with worry as she answered.

'I came to Grianan Ailech when I heard that a Formorian vessel had been sighted on the seas. The Druids do not consider the Formorians a threat but I remember the ancient stories of pillage and piracy. If this conquered race is planning to rise up, my people must be ready to fight them.'

'The Druids are concerned with matters greater than piracy,' Radarc said.

Banba's voice was bitter. 'And as ever they do not inform the Queen of such matters. Today a message came from the Council calling forth warriors to their hosting-places. The men ride to the House of a Thousand Warriors, the women to the Hill of Female-Warriors, draining this fortress of its strength. No reasons were given me but I know this means that war is stirring. And now worst of all ill tidings,' the Queen's eyes filled with tears, 'you tell me that Eriu is to die. I wish with all my heart that I had not lived to see this day. My reign closes in ruin and night is upon us.'

Banba lowered her head to weep. Aherne moved to approach her but Kay held the girl back. The two had stayed by the passageway as Radarc conferred with the Queen, but while Aherne listened with sympathy to their talk, Kay had been surveying the room with shrewd eyes. Not finding what she sought, she finally spoke up.

'Do you have the royal sword?'

The Queen stopped crying abruptly and seemed to notice Kay and Aherne for the first time. Her tear-stained face frowned at the two hooded strangers who stood in the shadow of the doorway. She looked at Radarc as if he should explain but Kay stepped forward and bowed politely.

'Queen Banba, I'm sorry to be rude but my friend and I are on a quest that might help your land. We're looking for a sword which should be here. I think it could be the one that you hold as sovereign.'

Whether she believed what Kay said, or her distraught state affected her judgement, the Queen did not ask questions but answered truthfully.

'The Sword is not with me. I sent it to the Druids this very evening at their request.'

Aherne let out a low cry and Kay's voice echoed her confusion.

'Too late? But we . . . I saw it in the Brugh . . . I don't understand. It can't be the right one then. Does it have a diamond blade? And a hilt . . .'

Banba was already nodding. Kay's heart sank.

'Who are you? And what is this quest you speak of?' the Queen demanded.

Kay was about to reply when a great uproar in the citadel ended all discussion.

Red shadows flared against the walls of the Queen's bower. Through the window came a cacophony of shouts, crashing noises and a heavy booming sound. The Queen was up in an instant, her travails forgotten as the discipline of rule took over. She ran to the window, the others close behind. They looked down on a scene of turmoil and terror.

The stillness of the night had been shattered as if the furies were unleashed upon Grianan Ailech. Fires were burning everywhere. People ran wildly. Cries of pain and panic mingled with shouts of command. Descending through the air like deadly rain were missiles of flaming straw. And over the noise of mayhem came the ominous sound of a battering ram as it struck the gate.

Banba's face was grim.

'We cannot withstand an attack. Only a handful of warriors remain in the citadel. There is nothing we can do but flee to the walls and hope that some may survive.' She turned to Radarc. 'Go now and take your companions with you. I must stay by my people.'

'You cannot stay, Banba,' Radarc said in a quiet but compelling tone. 'It is not the will of the Goddess that the Queen should die. Neither you nor I can disobey Her. My prey is not in this fortress and I must ride again but I will take you with me to safety.'

Not waiting for her protests, the Sentinel took the Queen by the arm and led her through the opening into the secret passageway. Kay and Aherne followed quickly behind and pulled the block of stone back into place. Once again they were moving through darkness but now haste made them scrape their hands and faces against the hard walls.

When they came out of the tunnel they were met with chaos. The attackers had broken through the gate and were flooding into Grianan Ailech with weapons brandished. The Danaan warriors who manned the walls ran to meet them. Swords clashed in furious combat but the Danaans were hopelessly outnumbered and could not stem the onslaught. The enemy poured into the citadel. Their wild cries rang through the burning night, followed by the sickening sounds of murder and destruction.

Kay and Aherne were pressed against the wall, hemmed in by the surging crowd of pursuer and pursued. Radarc had made his way to the gate, stone dagger drawn, Banba in the shelter of his arm. He turned quickly when he realized that the girls were not with him and cried out to them.

'To me, companions! To the *feth fiada!*'

It was impossible. Cut off by the stream of attackers, Kay and Aherne were pushed even further back by the Danaans who were fleeing to the refuge of the tunnel. Kay saw the flash of grief in the Sentinel's eyes before he and the Queen disappeared behind the veil of his power. But his voice rang out.

'Courage, little ones! The mark of the Goddess is upon you!'

The girls were terrified by the scenes around them. Men dying in pools of blood. Women dragged screaming out of the citadel. Clinging to each other, they struggled against the mob in an attempt to return to the safety of the passageway. But they were pushed further and further away till at last they broke free, stumbling into a narrow alley. It was a brief respite, however, as they found themselves surrounded by a band of armed men.

There was no time to flee, no time for Kay to try and use her power. The men rushed forward to heave them over burly shoulders. The next thing they knew they were being rushed out of the fortress, part of the booty of a roaring horde.

Upside down, winded by the rough handling, Kay and Aherne had no notion of where they were going. The ground sped past them as the stocky legs of their captors plunged downwards from the summit of Grianan Ailech. All around came the heavy sounds of men running and the muffled weeping of captured women. There was no order to the charge, yet all moved in the same direction. It was only when they were brusquely dropped to the ground that they could see what lay ahead.

The wide bay of Swiligh shone before them, bathed in moonlight. Upon its waters, floating like sleeping gulls, were slender ships curved from prow to stern. The raiders were splashing through the shallows and flinging their plunder aboard—weapons and gold, cloths and foodstuffs. Kay and Aherne were pushed towards one of the ships and thrown on board. The men jumped in behind them, rushing to the benches to thrust out the long oars. The ship moved swiftly under the hands of the rowers. As the coast fell away behind them and the wind rose with a cold ferocity, they knew they were heading for open sea.

Huddled in the bottom of the boat, Kay peered through the dimness at the men who had captured her. They were thick-bearded and cloaked in fur, and their metal helmets glittered with pointed horns. They looked like Vikings but that was hardly possible. Their ancestors perhaps? Were these the invaders of Inisfail?

They were now crossing the white-capped sea. As the oars were pulled in, a great square sail was unfurled. Upon its billowing surface a painted emblem glared: a single red eye that spouted flame.

'The Formorians!' Aherne cried. Her voice rang with hatred and despair.

Chapter Ten

THE VOYAGE WAS ROUGH and wild. Mountainous waves crashed against the ship and flung icy spray over the bows. The vessel rode the flooded waters like a bucking stag, climbing over the swells to rush down again. The white moon shone on the frosty foam. The stars drowned in the cold rim of the sea.

The ship was long and strongly timbered, broad within and high-sided but open to the elements. Unsheltered from the blasts of wind and water, the girls sat crouched together, cloaks wrapped tightly around them. The terror of the night and the torturous cold kept them wide awake. There was little comfort in the howl of the wind, the creaking of the ship and the snap of the sail that flew overhead. They were sailing through darkness to a darker unknown.

Kay's mind raced in circles. What are we going to do now? Where are they taking us? Why is this happening?

As if following her thoughts, Aherne murmured hopelessly.

'The quest is far behind us now. We are lost.'

'Don't give up yet,' Kay whispered. 'If they intended to kill us they would have done it already.'

Reassured by her own words, Kay stared curiously at their captors. With the sail unfurled, the men had settled down to rest, some sleeping with loud snores, others talking quietly among themselves. They seemed oblivious of their prisoners who cowered in silence amongst the booty. All women, Kay noted with an anxious pang.

One of the men began to sing, his voice rising above the roar of wind and sea. As he sang out a plaintive strain, the others joined in.

> Farewell to the cliffs of my homeland so fair
> Farewell to the island that I love so dear
> I must go upon the sea waves
> As the gull flies from the shore
> And leave all grief behind me
> Leave my home for evermore.
>
> I see ships departing out on the sea
> The white sails of freedom beckon to me
> I hear the wind sighing
> And I must go away
> For in this land of sorrow
> My people cannot stay.

Kay was affected by the strength of feeling in the song and she let her mind reach out to touch the men. The images that came to her were violent and horrific. Pictures of murder and cruelty, pestilence and starvation. Behind the images, she could sense the shadow of some inescapable evil.

Their evil or someone else's? Kay wondered. She probed further.

A rocky desolate place. A small gathering of people, tall and silver-haired like the men aboard the ship. Their backs were bent in labour, men, women and children. All toiled at some great endeavour. But they were so few in number. Kay could feel the hardship of their striving. At last she caught an image of their goal. A tower of glittering crystal.

'Who are these people?' she whispered to Aherne. 'Are they the invaders the Druids were talking about?'

Aherne's face twisted with contempt as she glared at the rows of men. She was pale and shivering from the cold but her animosity fired her with energy.

'They could not be! They would not dare! They are only the miserable remnants of a conquered tribe. Sea rovers. Pirates. Lower than beasts. We defeated the Formorians over a thousand years ago at the Second Battle of Moytura and we have all but extinguished their race.'

Kay frowned. She didn't like what Aherne was saying, but she knew so little about the history of this land that she was unwilling to make judgements.

'If it was over a thousand years ago,' she said quietly, 'they must have recovered by now. Obviously they have, or we wouldn't be here.'

'This I cannot understand!' Aherne spat out. 'The few who survived were banished to the island of Torinis, their former stronghold. The Druids cursed them with sickness and plague. Grianan Ailech was built as the northern guard. War and disease have always kept them down. How could they have risen again?'

A sick feeling came over Kay as she listened to her companion. The Formorian song and the images she had seen were suddenly understandable. Memories from Kay's own time rose to haunt her and she could no longer remain neutral.

'Are you talking about *genocide*?'

The revulsion in Kay's face shocked Aherne. It was like a mirror reflecting back to her a view she had never seen, an opinion she had never considered.

'They are the enemy,' Aherne insisted but her tone was defensive.

'For a thousand years?' Kay argued. 'That's crazy. No, it's worse. You already defeated them. What about peace treaties and reconstruction and . . .' She stopped when she saw Aherne's blank look, then shook her head unhappily. 'It's wrong. No matter who's doing it or why. It's wrong.'

The two were quiet after that, each struggling with her own thoughts and doubts. Kay's opinion made sense to Aherne, yet it condemned the very belief and behaviour of her tribe. Kay herself was facing a painful dilemma. If the Tuatha De Danaan were guilty of murdering another race, why was she trying to help them? She had taken for granted that the quest was a good one, that she was on 'the right side.'

Now she wasn't so sure.

Such disturbing thoughts only worsened the misery of that voyage and the two girls endured the hours in brooding silence.

A sudden flurry of activity warned them that they were approaching land. The sail was furled speedily as the oars slid over the gunnels to splash into the water. Before them loomed a large island with jagged cliffs that sheered upwards from the surging sea. For a moment it looked as if the ship were heading directly for the rocks but the coastline opened abruptly into a tiny cove.

'Torinis,' Aherne said in a low voice to Kay. 'Once they had a tower . . .'

Kay stiffened. 'What kind of tower?'

'The Tower of Conaing, it was called. A tor of shining crystal. When we defeated Balor Strongsmiter at the Battle of Moytura, my people razed it to the ground.'

'What was it for?' Kay asked, remembering her images. She knew the tower was important, perhaps the key to what the Formorians planned to do.

Aherne shrugged. 'The legends say that from the top of the tower the Formorians were able to see all the lands of the world.'

'They've built it again.'

'That is not possible,' Aherne said adamantly. 'The Druids would not allow it.'

'I think the Druids have been slipping for a few years now,' was Kay's reply.

As they neared the island shore, the men jumped from their ships with the eagerness of those who had arrived home. Straining and shouting, they pulled the vessels through the shallows to beach them on the pebbly sand. The captives were herded together, the plunder heaved onto strong backs, and the raiding party set off across the island.

In the darkness of night Torinis looked a desperate place, a craggy outcrop in the sullen sea. Part bog, part stone, the ground they were treading was difficult and treacherous. They clambered over the rocks, moving upwards towards the north-eastern tip of the island. The winds whipped them mercilessly. They could hear the sea pounding the cliffs below. As they climbed higher, Kay grabbed hold of Aherne.

'There!' she hissed.

A low noise issued from Aherne's throat.

Despite the gloom they could see it clearly, jutting out from the highest point of the island: a tower that pierced the sky like a silver spear.

Kay's eyes shone.

'Everything's okay,' she said softly. 'We're supposed to be here. I can *feel* it.'

Below the tower winked the yellow lights of a small settlement. The men shouted with triumph and drove their captives towards it. Kay and Aherne linked arms as they entered the village. The long timber houses had gabled roofs that curved downwards to the ground. In the lighted doorways stood the families of the raiders to greet and cheer them. The mood was celebratory as the welcoming crowd joined with the returning band. Together they thronged into the largest of the houses.

The hall had a sunken floor of hard earth. In the centre burned a great fire in a trough. Despite the opening in the low roof, the air was filled with stinging smoke. Narrow benches lined the walls alongside tables set on trestles. No wealth was evident and the weapons which hung from the rafters were crude and plain, but the wooden furniture was fancifully carved. Lamps of oil flared in soapstone bowls set on ledges above the hall.

The entire settlement was present, a noisy jubilant crowd. The people were tall of stature, all with the white hair and blue eyes of the Formorian race. The bearded men were clad in trousers of red and green tied with wide sashes. The women wore pleated dresses with oval brooches on their shoulders and hair braided in plaits. With fair skin reddened by wind and salt air, they looked a hardy people, bred on an island in the sea. But Kay guessed their number to be a mere hundred or two. How could they hope to invade Inisfail?

The captives were brought before the high table where a woman stood waiting, a giantess with hair of silver that fell in braids to her waist. She was slim but muscular, clothed in a red gown with a heavy fur vest. Her long white arms were bare except for the bronze hands that twisted like serpents above her elbows. Upon her head was a metal helmet with horns of ivory like the cusps of the moon. A great dagger hung on a cord around her neck. She had a fierce and awesome face, deathly white with lips blood-red. Her eyes were as cold as the sea as she glared down at the captured women.

'Hear me, women of the Tuatha De Danaan. You have been brought to Torinis for a noble purpose. Long has your race laboured to destroy mine but I, Liag Finehair, descendant of Balor Strongsmiter, tell you now—the Formorians will never die.

'With our own strength and will to survive we have overcome the curses you laid upon us. And as your eyes grew weaker and you failed to keep watch, we built our ships again.

'Once the Formorians were a great people of the sea. Your race has left us small and weak. But we shall thrive again and *you* will help us. You will be wives to Formorian men and bear Formorian children. This is tribute rightfully imposed. Since your race has given us naught but death, you in turn will bring us new life. Your blood will mix with ours. Learn our ways. You are now Formorian.'

A wail rose up from the Danaan women, yet it was one of loss not terror. Each wept that she faced exile from her home and people, but each also was relieved to discover that she was not about to die.

With a wave of her hand Liag ordered the women removed from the hall, but Kay spoke up quickly.

'Great Queen, I can help you in other ways.'

Kay's heart was racing madly but she forced herself to appear calm. She knew it was time to take command of the situation and she knew also that she had the power to do it. From the moment she had seen the Tower of Conaing she had felt it—a nameless force strengthening her mind. She understood, without knowing how or why, that the source of this power was compelling her to act.

Kay saw Liag's anger rise and quickly reached out to touch the woman's mind. So much easier now, the connection was instant, like opening a window onto an unknown landscape. And with the closeness and ease of that viewing, Kay sensed she could do more. Slowly, tentatively she insinuated herself into the pictures of Liag's mind, walking quietly through the halls of the woman's own memory.

Liag's eyes widened with shock and fear. Kay broke her concentration.

'Are you a sorceress?' Liag demanded, recovering quickly with an effort of will.

'I have power,' Kay said, bowing her head. 'And this girl is my apprentice.'

Aware that something had happened between Liag and Kay, Aherne hid her surprise and bowed also. She grinned secretively at Kay as the two of them were released while the other women were led away.

'Come dine with me,' Liag said, pushing the men near her out of their seats. 'We shall talk as sisters,' and she forced a smile on the girls.

Kay shuddered inwardly. The smile of a cobra. She would have to be careful with this formidable woman.

Kay and Aherne sat on either side of Liag as the Formorians settled down to their victory feast. Wooden platters were brought to the tables heaped with mussels, clams, sausage and cheese curds. A cheer resounded through the hall as meat stolen from Grianan Ailech was carried to the fire on a spit. Everything tasted of onion and garlic. To wash the food down there were great cups of cattle-horn brimming with a thick malted beer. There was no music or dancing but a heavy-set bard recited a poem of praise while the warriors displayed their plunder to the crowd.

Kay felt herself sinking with fatigue as she tried to eat the heavy meal but, though she ached for sleep, she forced herself to stay sharply awake. She needed a clear head to deal with Liag who had already begun her deadly questioning.

'What use to me are your powers, my dear?'

Again Kay entered Liag's mind though she hid her presence this time. She sifted through the images like a sheaf of photographs, but was unable to find anything that would help her answer the question.

'You've built the Tower of Conaing again,' Kay said, stalling for time.

Liag stuffed a piece of meat in her mouth and the juice trickled down her chin like blood. She wiped it away with the back of her hand.

'You saw the tower when you were brought here tonight. Do you take me for a fool? Beware, sorceress. I could kill you with my bare hands. You must prove your worth to me.'

Kay concentrated on Liag again and caught a single image that carried a weight of emotion in its wake. A fleet of ships sailing from Torinis. She hazarded a wild guess.

'You're leaving,' she said, afraid to say more.

It was enough. Liag stopped eating. She had begun to breathe quickly though she tried to hide her excitement.

'For *where*?' she demanded.

Kay was stiff with tension. She knew she was close but she had no idea what she was nearing. Liag's mind was blank on this point. Kay was mystified. Were the Formorians planning to invade Inisfail? But if they were, why didn't the images show her that? Unable to sort out the puzzle, Kay decided to bluff, acting as if she were in a trance.

'A place seen from the Tower of Conaing,' she intoned.

Liag let out a wild cry that made the girls jump. Her hard features were overcome with joy.

'The old tales are true! The tower *will* show me where to lead my people.'

It was then that Kay realized the truth she had stumbled upon and she remembered the song the men had sung aboard ship. The Formorians were leaving their homeland forever, not only Torinis but Inisfail as well. They were not invading the Tuatha De Danaan, they were escaping from them. That was why they had built the tower again, their ancient and traditional guide to the world.

Kay felt a pang of sympathy for the ruthless Liag. This woman had undoubtedly waged a long and terrible struggle to raise up her crippled tribe. Now with a last gasp of strength, she had raided those who were the cause of her tragedy, not for revenge but for supplies and new blood. And the building of the tower. A momentous feat for a decimated race. All for the purpose of finding a safe haven. But the tower was not finished, it seemed. It had yet to show them their new country.

Encouraged by her success, Kay tried a long shot.

'And the invader will help you finish the tower in return for your support.'

'Invader? What invader?'

Liag's surprise came too swiftly not to be genuine. Too late Kay realized her mistake. Liag of the Formorians, single-mindedly bent on her own plans, knew nothing of the doom facing her ancient enemy. Kay had opened a box that was better left closed.

When Liag saw the girl flounder, her eyes narrowed suspiciously.

'Have you been trying to deceive me? Do you not have foresight? *Who is this invader you speak of?*'

Kay's stomach churned. Here was a question she couldn't hope to answer but if she admitted that, she would lose Liag's confidence. Her bluff had been called and she knew she was in trouble. She caught a new image from Liag's angry mind. Her own death was mirrored there like a dark threat.

Chapter Eleven

KAY WAS SEARCHING FRANTI-
cally for a response to Liag when both were distracted by a
commotion in the hall. Two Formorian warriors were dragging
a prisoner towards the head table. The captive was a young
man, dark-haired and slight of build. Though he had been
badly beaten he was putting up a valiant struggle.

'We found him at the tower,' one of the guards reported
gruffly to Liag. 'He refuses to speak.'

The prisoner was pushed forward, a sword at his back. His
clothes were torn and spattered with blood and his face was
bruised, but despite his appearance there was about him an
air of fineness and nobility. He had a mane of hair that fell in
thick curls to his shoulders; his features were dark and
smooth. He glared defiantly at Liag. Everything in his stance
implied that had he had a weapon he would continue to
fight.

Aherne stared at his proud carriage, the dark eyes, the curls
of hair, and her heart tightened with a peculiar twist.

'He does not have the colouring of a Danaan lord,' Liag
said. 'Who are you, stranger?'

When the prisoner remained silent, Liag left the table and
strode up to him. She was a good deal taller and he winced in
pain as she grasped his wounded shoulders.

'You will answer soon enough, my boy. You will tell us why you are on Torinis or you will die.'

The two guards were quick and eager to their duty. One held his sword to the fire till it glowed like a rod of molten metal. The other forced the stranger to his knees and tore the clothing from his back.

'No, no,' Aherne moaned, as she saw the slim back bowed to the ground. The muscles were held taut in anticipation of the torture but he did not plead or struggle. Aherne leaned across the table to catch Kay's arm. 'You must stop this!'

'I can't,' Kay said helplessly.

She didn't have the power to overcome the entire hall. She could do nothing for this courageous and unfortunate man.

'A little at a time,' Liag was saying coolly. 'I want him conscious.'

A scream tore from the prisoner's unwilling throat as the hot blade rested against his skin.

Kay felt faint with horror. Her mind raced to think of something she could do. But another cry followed after the prisoner's and from the corner of her eye she saw a flash of green as Aherne leaped over the table.

Head lowered, Aherne charged the Formorian guard like a bull, striking his stomach with the force of a blow. He fell backwards, his sword clattering to the ground. For one instant everyone froze with surprise. Only two people were fully aware of what happened. Aherne who stood over the prisoner, her eyes shining with concern, and the stranger himself who stared up at her with admiration and gratitude. Then the hall erupted. Kay stood up in panic. Liag screamed with rage. More guards rushed forward to take hold of Aherne and the prisoner.

'To the pit!' Liag roared, pointing to Kay as well.

As Kay was dragged past her, Liag spoke with relentless fury.

'Three deaths tomorrow will mark the last stones of the Tower of Conaing.'

The three were taken from the hall and dragged out of the village to be thrown into a dark pit cut into the ground. With metal bars overhead, the cold damp prison was open to the night.

The stranger was now unconscious. Quickly the girls bent over him, binding the worst of his wounds with cloth torn from their blouses. Then they wrapped their cloaks around him like a warm cocoon.

'I am sorry for my rashness,' Aherne said to Kay as they worked. 'It is my fault we are here. But I could not bear to see them torture him.'

'I thought you were great,' Kay said. 'You were like a warrior! And besides,' she added ruefully, 'you saved me from Liag. Thanks to my big mouth we could've been in worse trouble.'

'What could be worse than this?' Aherne said, looking around the pit.

Water trickled from the ground above and ran over the green slime that oozed in the porous rock.

Kay shrugged with sudden humour. 'Well, at least we have the rest of the night to figure out our escape.'

'Not the rest of the night, *please*?' Aherne said with a mock groan, picking up Kay's mood.

Despite the chill, the dark and the threat of their death the next day, the two burst into laughter. They were still laughing when they realized that the stranger had woken and was staring at them in amazement.

'What manner of women are you,' he said hoarsely, 'that you laugh in the face of death?'

'Idiots, I should think,' Kay said with an amused snort. She was feeling strangely elated.

Aherne leaned over the man to ease his head against the hard ground. Her voice was gentle.

'No braver than you,' she said.

'Then we are a fine match,' he replied, staring into her eyes.

Aherne looked away, her face colouring.

Kay raised her eyebrows at the two of them. Her good humour was rapidly increasing. This was hardly the setting for a romance but one seemed to be unfolding in front of her.

'Will you tell us who you are?' Kay asked him.

The stranger looked wary.

'You don't have to if you don't want to,' Kay said. 'It makes no difference to us. We're going to escape. We could help you too, but if you don't trust us . . .'

The man smiled a slow smile of respect for her tactics.

'Lady, I am sworn to secrecy as to who I am and where I come from but I will tell you my name. I am Amergin, son of Milidh.'

Kay frowned as the name was somehow familiar. Then Amergin spoke again as he raised himself painfully on his elbows.

'I am grateful for what you have done but indeed if you are able to free yourselves I would suggest you go without me. I am in no condition to travel and would only hinder you dangerously.'

'You have a point there,' Kay said but she saw Aherne's face fall.

Kay sighed as she tried to sort out the situation. She drew Aherne away, to the far side of the pit.

'We're back on the quest and in the right place,' she said to the girl's surprise. 'It's the only explanation for what I've been feeling. Fintan said the treasures had power of their own and something's been strengthening the two of us. One of the treasures must be on this island.'

'But we are here by pure chance!' Aherne protested. 'It was the Brugh and Grianan Ailech we were directed to, not Torinis. If the Formorians had not raided . . .'

Kay made an impatient noise. 'And if you and I hadn't been born we would never have met. There are too many coincidences. And Fintan told us that as well. If we seek with our hearts and our instincts for the true, *the treasures will find us*. Crazy as it sounds, I believe one of them has been calling to me.'

Aherne bit her lip as she tried to absorb what Kay was saying but her eyes and attention kept straying to Amergin. He was lying back again, staring up at the moon that shone through the bars of their prison.

'And what about him?' Aherne asked.

'What about him,' said Kay.

'My instinct says we should help him,' Aherne insisted, though she was flustered by Kay's look. 'It would not be right to leave him to die, even if he does hinder us.'

'I agree,' Kay said to Aherne's obvious relief. 'But we'll have to come back for him. He wouldn't be able to climb the tower.'

'Climb the tower!' Aherne said aghast, then she stopped as the realization dawned on her. 'Ah yes. If the Formorians have one of our treasures, there would be no better place to keep it.'

Kay grinned. 'I'm glad you can still think even when your mind's on something else.'

Amergin said nothing when they explained they would return before morning. He motioned to them to take their cloaks but they refused. With a final glance at Aherne, he closed his eyes.

'He doesn't believe we are coming back,' Aherne said sadly.

'He'll know the truth soon enough,' Kay replied. She was frowning up at the bars. 'Now all we have to do is get out of here.'

Kay's confidence in her power was growing steadily, but she was still unsure of its abilities and extent. Not for the first time she wished someone had taught her how to use it, instead of her having to discover everything by herself.

She reached out with her mind beyond the prison and sensed two men sitting nearby.

'Sentries!' she thought anxiously, but as their minds opened to her easily she realized what she could do.

She sent them strong images like a sleeping draught: birds with their heads tucked beneath the soft underfeathered wing; mice sleeping deeply in the burrows of the earth; men lost in dreams under the warm blankets of night. She chuckled when the loud snores reached her in the pit.

'That wasn't too hard,' she congratulated herself. 'But we're still locked up.'

The bars above were thick and solid, set firmly in place. The guards had lifted them up when the prisoners were thrown into the pit, but it would be impossible to move them from underneath. If just one was loosened, however, there would be room enough for the girls to escape.

Kay stared at the rock that held the bars in place. If it were only human she would be able to touch it with her mind. Her heart leaped suddenly. Could she perhaps? Could she actually use her power on inanimate things?

'Mind over matter,' she told herself hopefully.

Concentrating with all the effort she could muster, Kay imagined the rock crumbling around one of the bars. Even as she strained with that single-minded idea, she could sense the stone resisting with the stubborn force of inertia.

'Come on, come on,' she commanded furiously. 'You'll have to erode sometime,' and she thought of the wind and the rain and the sea, the natural enemies of immovable rock.

At last it began to work. In small bits at first and then with increasing speed, the rock wore down till it streamed to the floor like sand.

'I did it!' Kay said with triumph as Aherne stared in wonder. 'I wasn't sure I could do it, but I did!'

Aherne laughed with delight, sharing her friend's excitement.

'Your power is growing. We are lucky. The quest would be lost without it.'

'So let's get going,' Kay said happily. 'You climb on my back and remove the bar. Then help me up as soon as you're out.'

Though the bar was loosened, it wasn't easy to push it aside. The two girls almost fell as Aherne strained precariously on her friend's slight shoulders. But when the metal rod finally gave way, Aherne heaved herself upwards onto the edge of the pit. She reached down for Kay who had begun to scale the wall.

Out of the prison they were struck by the biting wind as their torn blouses gave them no protection. They moved quickly to set the bar back in place, then stepped in silence past the sleeping guards.

Neither Kay nor Aherne saw the relief in Amergin's eyes as the two made good their escape. Nor did they hear him whisper sadly to himself.

'Farewell, sweet one. I hope we shall meet again.'

He stared patiently up at the sky, ignoring the pain of his body. He knew his people would find him before the night was through. He wished he could have said as much to those bright and courageous young women. At least then they would have taken their cloaks. A pang of remorse added to his physical discomfort. Yet it was best that they left before his own men came. He would have had difficulty protecting them, especially if the fair girl revealed her strange powers. He sighed. Ah, but it was the red-haired warrior he would dream of for days to come.

CHAPTER TWELVE

KAY AND AHERNE HAD NO
trouble deciding which way they were headed. Their prison pit
was a long way from the Formorian village but not far from the
promontory where the Tower of Conaing stood. The tower
rose up beyond them like a beam of light, a crystal pendant
hanging from the black throat of the sky. They ran towards it,
stumbling over the rocky ground, urged on by the fear of
approaching dawn. Though it had been a long day and an even
longer night, neither felt tired. They were both strangely
refreshed, ready and eager to find the first treasure.

When they reached the base of the tower, they stared up at
it in awe. They had had no idea of its size as it stood against the
limitless horizon of sea and sky, but now it seemed to touch the
very stars. Circular at its foundation, it tapered as it rose, block
upon block of sparkling quartz. It was not for fortification or
war. Steps were hewn on the outside of the tower, coiling
upwards like a serpent. And a great door opened on the
ground.

'They're building from the centre,' Kay said, as she peered
through the door. The inside was immense like a marble cathe-
dral. Wooden scaffolding loomed upwards, dangling with long
pulleys of hemp. Blocks of stone lay scattered about, waiting to
be lifted.

'Such incredible work for a small number of people,' Aherne murmured.

The girls climbed the narrow stairway on the outside of the tower, circling round and round. The height made them dizzy and stiff with cold. They couldn't decide which was worse, facing outwards to the ever-increasing drop below or inwards to the wall with no support at their backs. In the end each chose differently. Aherne faced the tower, unable to stomach the view behind her, while Kay turned outwards, her back pressed to the cold stone, bravely defying the breadth of land-scape below.

By the time they reached the top, the tower had narrowed to a circle the size of a small house, still awaiting the final blocks of stone. The girls leaned their arms on the ledge and looked around them.

'This is heady stuff,' said Kay.

They could see the full shape of the island, a sickle of rock dropped into an infinity of sea. It was a bleak and thrilling sight: craggy cliffs suffering the onslaught of ceaseless waves; rock-strewn perches and high eyries where the seabirds slept; tracts of stony ground and treeless wastes.

'Good!' she said softly, as she looked towards the west.

Far far beyond, across thousands of miles of ocean, she could see the thin glimmer of another land. And she had used only a moment of her power. The tower itself had done the rest. She was happy for the Formorian race. They *would* see their new country when the work was finished. That would be tomorrow, as Liag had told her three prisoners when she condemned them to death. Remembering that threat brought Kay back to the task at hand.

She turned from the vast scene around her and looked towards the centre of the tower. A space of a few feet separated the wooden scaffolding from the wall, room for the blocks to be pulled into place.

Aherne was gazing down into the depths below.

'They are brave workers,' she muttered, forgetting that she was speaking of a hated race.

'There it is!' Kay cried suddenly, pointing with excitement. 'We've found the *Spear*!'

At the farthest corner of the scaffolding was a little table covered with fine cloth. It was obviously an altar set up by the Formorians to appeal to the gods in their great endeavour. It held votive offerings and sacred objects, but one stood out from the others. A tall spear with a shaft of ivory and a diamond point that shone like blue-white fire.

A low hum rang through Kay's mind like the echo of some ancient song.

'I can feel its power,' she said breathlessly. 'It *was* the source that strengthened us.'

'I do not have that strength now,' Aherne said and her voice quavered.

Kay looked at her with concern. The younger girl stared with fixed horror at the space between the tower and the scaffolding. The drop below was like a gaping mouth, but it would have to be crossed for the sake of the treasure.

'I cannot abide heights,' Aherne said, leaning weakly against the ledge. 'It was not easy coming up here and now worse is called for. I . . . I cannot move. It is as if every moment of cowardice has gathered together to defeat me.'

'It's okay. Don't worry,' Kay said gently, putting her arm around the girl. 'Only one of us has to get it.'

Kay considered the distance she would have to jump. It wasn't that far and her legs were long. If she kept her head there was no reason to fail.

'Better do it now,' she told herself, 'before I lose my nerve thinking about it.'

She took a deep breath and pulled herself up onto the rim of the tower. She commanded her eyes to look only at the platform ahead and not at the fatal drop below. She swayed slightly, caught off guard by the winds that raged around her, but before she could lose her balance she made her jump.

In the dark leap forward and those terrifying seconds, Kay suddenly knew that she wasn't going to make it. She screamed in panic as she fell short of her mark, reaching out just in time to grip the edge of the scaffold.

Aherne held her breath as Kay jumped, then let it out again with a wild cry. She didn't stop to think. There was no time to hesitate. Her fear fled in the overwhelming need to save Kay. She heaved herself onto the ledge then hurled herself forward with all her might. A flash of black sky above and dark ground below, then she landed safely in a sprawl on the other side. The wind was knocked out of her but she whirled around, still gasping for breath, to grab hold of Kay's wrists. Kay's eyes stared up at her, wild with shock and terror, as she clung to the scaffold with taut white hands.

'Stay with me! Stay with me!' Aherne cried, her face wet with tears.

Kay could feel the tight grip of the other girl and the pure force of will that was exerted behind it.

Slowly they moved, in cautious unison, hand gripping arm, arms gripping shoulders, then a final heave from the waist. At last both tumbled backwards onto the platform.

They wept and hugged each other with wordless relief. It was some time before either was able to recover. Then Kay wiped her eyes with some semblance of calm.

'I guess that's how it had to happen. We had to earn the Spear together.'

With silent awe, and almost reverent formality, they lifted the Spear from the Formorian altar. It was a special moment. After all their efforts and misadventures, they had finally gained a treasure! Both could feel its power tingle through them like sap rising in the trees to the call of Spring. But they couldn't linger. Dawn was near and they had to make good their escape.

Descending the tower was even more harrowing than climbing it. Neither wanted to attempt another jump to reach the stairway. Instead they moved slowly down the platform, clinging precariously to the rungs of the scaffold. But though they had to carry the Spear across their shoulders it turned out to be a help rather than a hindrance. Both could feel the treasure feeding them energy to increase their speed and agility as well as their courage.

When they reached the ground they hurried towards the rocky pit as the first rays of morning crept over the sky.

They knew something was wrong as soon as they came within sight of the pit. The metal rods had been torn up and thrown aside. Aherne raced forward.

'They have taken him!' she cried, kneeling at the edge of the prison. 'We should not have left him!'

'It's not what you think,' Kay said.

She pointed gravely to the bloodstained ground and the signs of a fierce battle.

'Someone rescued Amergin.'

'I'm glad of that,' said Aherne, though she sounded disappointed. She would have preferred to have rescued him herself.

'Let's get out of here,' Kay urged, 'before the Formorians come looking for us.'

'Back to the cove where the ships are?' Aherne suggested.

Kay nodded. 'We've got to get off this island somehow. I'm hoping the Spear's power will help us do it.'

'Oh, for some food and warmth and a good night's sleep,' Aherne groaned as they set off once again across the rocky terrain. 'I would have eaten more of that barbarous food if I had known what was in store for us.'

'Me too,' Kay said, trying to ignore her empty stomach. 'Serves us right for being picky. Go with the flow, as they say in my time.'

But though they were hungry and cold and tired, the two were in high spirits. They were free once again and had a treasure in their possession at last.

They made a detour around the village to retrace the path they had taken the night before. They moved quickly and stealthily, aware that at any moment a clamour could erupt, signalling the discovery of the prisoners' escape. The cover of night had yielded to grey dawn. The dim landscape of the island was harsh and grim. When they reached the cove where the long ships lay beached, they were relieved to find it unguarded.

They chose a small boat and pushed it into the water.

'I know nothing of seafaring,' Aherne said, as they scrambled aboard. She glanced uneasily at the arched prow carved in the shape of a serpent's head. The great teeth of a sea beast snarled in its jaw.

Kay was also viewing the ship with alarm. The tiller was in the stern, thrusting crosswise into the vessel and attached to a rudder that worked from the side. The very simplicity of the design warned her that the sailors themselves relied on unique skills and instinct.

'I've got my power and the Spear as well,' she assured herself. 'If I could use it on the rock in the prison pit, there's no reason why it shouldn't work on the ship.'

She took her position in the stern, one hand on the tiller, the other gripping the Spear upright.

'Move,' Kay thought with quiet command. 'Move over the water.

The Spear shone like a torch, she could feel it strengthening her concentration. As the ship moved away from the shore, Kay called to Aherne to loosen the sheets. The girl shinnied up the mast to tug at the lines till the sail billowed free. The red eye of the Formorians glared balefully down as they sailed from Torinis.

Sunrise was flooding the sky to set the sea afire in waves of red and purple-blue. Though the light was like a warm breath on their faces, they were chilled by the seaborne winds and the clinging spray. Out beyond them raged the wild ocean.

'I wish we had our cloaks,' Aherne said, shivering where she sat at Kay's feet.

The older girl said nothing as she stared out to sea. Her eyes were pale with the intensity of thought. The Spear was feeding her knowledge as well as strength. She could sense the unseen path that led from Torinis to the mainland and she guided the ship carefully in its wake.

But they were not long at sea when their voyage ended.

The other ship seemed to appear from nowhere, gliding over the water like a sea snake. As it bore swiftly down on them the girls saw that it wasn't a Formorian vessel, but there were no flags or markings of identity.

'Is it a Danaan ship?' Kay asked anxiously. The last thing they wanted was to be brought before the Druids.

Aherne shook her head. 'My people are not seafarers, but there is a third tribe that lives in Inisfail . . .'

Kay tried to speed their ship away but it was hopeless. The other ship was much bigger and faster. It was not unlike a galleon with its full rigging and dark wood. As it drew near, figures scrambled up the masts to lash the sails. From openings in the hull, long oars shot out and sliced through the water.

'The savage Firbolg could not craft such a vessel,' Aherne said with a tremor of premonition. 'If it is not Formorian it must belong to the invader!'

They had no choice but to sit and wait as the other ship drew alongside them. Metal hooks swung through the air to tear at the eye of the Formorian sail. As the girls' boat came to a shuddering halt, a rope ladder fell with a thump in front of them. Armed men came hurrying down it.

'Hello,' Kay said dryly, as the first man approached her. 'As you can see, we're a small crew.'

The man stopped in surprise, eyes wide as if he could not believe what he saw. Before him were two girls in torn and muddied clothing. One stood erect holding a shining weapon, while the other sat at her feet and looked up at him curiously. Neither girl showed fear, only a weary acceptance that they had been captured. They were obviously quite wet and cold. An older man, he found himself thinking unexpectedly of his daughters. A smile tugged at the corners of his mouth.

'You will be warmer in our ship,' he said with gruff kindness.

He reached for the Spear, but Kay clung to it fiercely.

'I do not want to kill you,' he said sternly, raising his sword. 'Obey me and you will not be harmed.'

Kay looked at the men behind him and then up at the faces that peered down from the other ship. She didn't know if she could use her power against so many and she was afraid to take the chance under threat of death. The man saw her hesitate and pulled the Spear from her hand. Before they could object any further, the girls were trundled up the ladder.

Orders were being shouted around them but Kay and Aherne were beyond caring. They were prisoners once again and after all their trouble they had lost the Spear. Exhausted and dispirited, they stood lost on the high deck as the Formorian vessel was set ablaze. Then the oars of the new ship were pulled in swiftly, as the coloured sails flew overhead once more. Kay had just noticed that both men and women were handling the ship when she and Aherne were led away.

They expected to be put in some miserable hold but found themselves instead in a richly furnished cabin. The mahogany walls curved with the line of the ship, dark wood rising from brightly coloured rugs. A brazier of alabaster burned with red coals and there was a big bed heaped with silken cushions. A table had been laid out as if awaiting them with smooth black dishes engraved with white designs. Tureens of spiced food bubbled on lighted stands. Jewelled goblets brimmed with wine.

The girls stared in astonishment. They had heard the key turn in the lock and knew they were prisoners. But what sort of prison was this?

'It's too good to be true,' Kay said suspiciously. 'It must be some kind of trap.'

Aherne was already at the table sampling the delicacies.

'It could be poisoned,' Kay said quickly, though her stomach was screaming for food.

'I shall not die hungry then,' Aherne said, filling up a plate.

Kay couldn't resist any longer. She joined her friend at the feast. They were still eating when the door of their cabin opened. It was the older man who had captured them and his face was now openly friendly.

'Baths and dry clothing for my ladies,' he announced with a grin.

Behind him came men with two great tubs of water and a woman carrying an armful of linen.

'Our captain sends his regards. He will visit you when you have rested.'

'Where is the Spear?' Kay demanded.

'It is with the captain. You are safe now. Sleep a while. All will be settled when he speaks with you.'

Again they were left alone and again they heard the door lock. Aherne gave Kay a mystified shrug and inspected the metal baths.

'It's hot!' she cried joyfully, dipping her hand in the water.

As if that made up her mind, she stripped off her clothes and eased herself into one of the tubs. She could feel the ache of her limbs disappearing in the heat.

Kay handed her the urn that was standing near the baths and smiled wryly as the girl cried out with pleasure. The sweet-smelling oil bubbled like soap.

'"Go with the flow,"' Aherne said, catching her friend's look. 'That was your advice.'

Kay couldn't help but laugh at that. She undressed and climbed into the other tub. But unlike Aherne she couldn't simply enjoy the luxuries. Her weary mind raced with the mystery before her. Were these people the invaders of Inisfail? And if they were, why were they being so kind to strangers?

Seeing her worried frown, Aherne said lightly, 'The captain will explain it all, no doubt.' She lathered her short hair with the scented oil and laughed playfully. 'I have yet to meet this man but I could easily love him.'

Aherne's comment set Kay's mind on a new track and everything suddenly made sense. If things hadn't happened so fast she would have guessed it sooner. She had already reached her conclusion when she glanced at the bed.

'Your words may be truer than you think,' she said to Aherne, nodding towards the linen left out for them.

There neatly folded amongst the towels and clothing were two patches of forest-green.

'Our cloaks!' Aherne cried happily. Then her face clouded with confusion. 'Amergin!' she whispered.

'It's Amergin all right,' said Kay. 'Which answers a few questions but raises even more.'

Chapter Thirteen

Kay and aherne ate in leisurely comfort the sumptuous meal which had been brought to their cabin. It was late afternoon and they were well rested from their sleep. They wore the lovely clothes which had been given to them. Aherne was in a dress of emerald silk with a gold-threaded vest that clung to her slim form. Kay wore a flowing gown of dark-blue satin with seed pearls at the hem and cuffs. Having slept at last they were none the worse for their adventuring. Both had the glow of sun and wind on their faces and their eyes were bright with the vigour of youth. Kay had combed out her long hair till it shone like pale honey. Aherne looked at it enviously, tugging at her own short curls.

'I do not know why it is like this,' she said sadly. 'I do not remember cutting it.'

Even as the girl spoke, Kay caught an image from her mind. Aherne weeping wildly as she slashed at her long hair with a dagger. It was to punish herself, Kay sensed, but why? What had she done?

'Has none of your memory come back yet?' Kay asked. 'I thought the treasure might help since it gave you new courage.'

Aherne's eyes darkened. She looked uneasy. It suddenly occurred to Kay that the girl might not want to remember.

Kay was puzzled but unwilling to probe further. She found Aherne's emotions too unstable to manage.

'Your hair will grow back again,' she said instead. 'But I wouldn't worry about it. You're still very beautiful.'

Aherne coloured a little and said nothing. They had not spoken of Amergin since the discovery of their cloaks. Aherne was trying to ignore the unpleasant possibility that he was one of the invaders of her land.

'Whoever these people are,' Aherne said with forced lightness, 'they have fine tastes. These clothes, this food. I have never eaten such meat. Delicious!'

'It's pork,' Kay said. 'Their favourite dish, if I remember rightly.'

Aherne's eyes widened.

'Do you know who they are?!'

Kay was pensive. 'I'm beginning to figure it out but it's not all that clear to me. Back in my own time I had some special books. One of the stories in the Irish ones was about your race and an invasion that took place. Things have been growing more familiar to me the longer I've been here, but I can't recall everything. It's different when you're actually *in* the story. I mean, it's not as easy to see what's happening.'

Her confusion was mirrored in Aherne's face but the girl was able to grasp part of her meaning.

'If you have foreknowledge . . .' Aherne began.

'Hindsight,' Kay corrected her.

'. . . then you know what is to come. Will the invasion succeed?'

Kay hesitated to answer as she knew how difficult it would be for Aherne. Yet she couldn't hide the truth.

'I'm sorry,' Kay said softly, 'but according to my stories the conquest of Inisfail is inevitable.' She flinched as Aherne's face collapsed with shock, then hurried to add, 'But whether your people are conquered, I don't really know. The stories were vague about what happened to the Tuatha De Danaan.'

Aherne was pale and her eyes burned with tears.

'It is a terrible thing to be vanquished. A glorious people laid low.'

Kay frowned. 'I understand how you feel and I know it's hard but . . .' she paused, torn between loyalty for Aherne and her own opinion on the matter.

'But what?' Aherne demanded with a flash of anger.

Kay's frown deepened. She didn't want an argument but it seemed likely. Now that they had been captured by the invaders, they were directly affected by the war that was brewing. They could hardly avoid discussing it.

'I've been thinking about this,' Kay began hesitantly. 'It looks to me as if your people aren't the best kind of rulers. I mean they're even planning to kill their own Queen. The Druids seem to be the real power in the country and I don't trust them, especially Fiss and Fokmar. The massacre of the Formorians I can only see as evil. And you've mentioned another race. The Firbolg? I imagine they haven't been treated well either.' She took a deep breath. 'I'm sorry, Aherne. You're my friend and I really care about you, but your tribe itself seems cruel and heartless to me. I can't say that I'm sad they'll be conquered.'

As Aherne listened to Kay her face changed from surprise to fury and from fury to doubt. She loved and trusted the one who was saying these terrible things to her and deep inside she recognized the truth. But it was a truth too personal and painful to accept. Her face cooled over like a mask. She turned her back on Kay as she finished her meal in silence.

Kay was relieved that they hadn't argued but she wasn't happy. She had a growing suspicion that the invasion was somehow linked to their quest. But if the girls were divided by the war, how could they continue the quest together?

They sat without speaking till Amergin himself entered their cabin. In his crimson tunic and mantle of silk he did not look like the unfortunate prisoner they had aided on Torinis. Around his neck glittered the sign of his royalty, a heavy torc of twisted gold. His hair fell in loose curls to his shoulders. Though bruises still marred his face, his dark features were striking. The brown eyes settled immediately on Aherne, but it was Kay who addressed him.

'Amergin, son of Milidh,' she said. 'King of . . . ?'

'Prince,' he said with a bow. 'My father is king. I am a prince of the Gaedil.'

'And an enemy of my people!' Aherne cried, unable to control her anger and her pain.

The prince didn't rise to her taunt. He looked unhappy and spoke with disarming honesty.

'Would that it were not so. I have no desire to be an enemy of yours. You are a Danaan woman, then, as I feared?'

'I am Aherne of the Tuatha De Danaan,' she said with a haughty tilt of her head. 'This is my friend, Kay.'

Amergin sat down heavily and stared at them with moody speculation.

'I have not forgotten your kindness to me and I always pay my debts. My people would want you killed if they knew who you were. I have told them you are Firbolg. They have yet to recognize the different races of Inisfail as I have done most of the advance scouting by myself.

'That is how I govern my unruly tribe,' he added with a rueful smile. 'I must always know more than they do.'

'Is that why you were at the Tower of Conaing alone?' Kay asked.

Amergin nodded and his face brightened. 'A feat of ingenuity that tower, the work of master builders. I admire the
Formorians. It was my intention to make an ally of their
barbarian queen, but I ruined my chances when I was brought
before her in a helpless state. I shall befriend them after the
conquest. I want a peaceful land.'

'You needn't worry about the Formorians,' Kay said help-
fully. She liked what the prince was saying and she ignored
Aherne's furious glance. 'They're leaving Inisfail for another
land far in the west. In fact, if they finished the tower yesterday
they've probably left already.'

'I regret their departure,' Amergin said with sincerity. 'They
would have added greatly to my people's skills.'

Kay grew quiet as she tried to piece together an understanding of the invasion. The Gaedil were the invading tribe,
the unknown enemy of the Tuatha De Danaan. The
Formorians were gone and obviously had no part in the
conquest. But there was one more race in Inisfail and Amergin
seemed to know them.

'If it was all right to tell your people that we're Firbolg,' Kay
said slowly, 'does that mean the Firbolg are on your side?'

Amergin gave her a look of respect.

'You are quick-minded, Lady. Indeed the Firbolg are my
allies. They will support my invasion of Inisfail and in return for
this I shall restore to them their former lands and freedoms.
They have suffered long under the Danaan yoke.'

That was the final straw for Aherne. Her fury exploded. She
jumped up with fists clenched and eyes blazing with hatred.

'I will not sit with the enemy of my people and listen to
the fate you plan for Inisfail. You cannot fool me with your
sweet words. You are an invader. A thief stealing into my
country, taking what is not yours, bringing destruction—'

'Sit down and shut up!' Kay ordered, losing her temper as well.

Aherne fell back on her chair with confusion and dismay.

Kay's voice rose as she argued her point.

'We've already talked about this. I told you the conquest is inevitable. There's no use screaming about something you can't change. You've got to find the courage to accept what's happening and to understand why. If Amergin can talk about peace and allies, then these things aren't impossible in your time. That means the Tuatha De Danaan *choose* to rule badly. Whether you like it or not, they're getting what they deserve.'

Aherne's shoulders shook. Tears streamed down her face at Kay's harsh words.

Now that she had said what was on her mind, Kay was sorry. She ran over to embrace her friend.

Aherne saw that Kay was upset as well and shook her head sadly.

'Do you see how difficult it is to stand against those you love? How can I be expected to deny my own people?'

'But don't you see?' Kay pleaded. 'We've got to recognize who's right and wrong and pick the right side, no matter how hard it is. Our instinct for the true, that's what Fintan said. Even if it means standing against those we love, we've got to do what's right or we'll never succeed in the quest.'

Aherne grew calmer. Her features deepened with thought.

'The quest,' she said softly, 'is my only hope in the darkness. The four ancient treasures belong to the Danaan tribe. Surely that means they will help us.' She stared at Kay. 'You say the invasion will succeed but also that the fate of my people is unknown. The quest must be linked to their destiny. With that belief, Kay, I will tell you now—I know my people are wrong but I still hold hope for them. That hope lies in the quest. I shall follow it no matter what it calls me to do.'

Kay smiled at the girl with love and encouragement. 'You're growing stronger all the time. If all else fails, we must not lose *hope*.' She hugged Aherne again before returning to her seat.

Amergin had remained quiet throughout the girls' talk. Though he wasn't sure what had happened, he was glad to see that Aherne was no longer suffering. He was surprised by his depth of feeling for the girl, but made no effort to counter it. It was her rash courage which had first impressed him but now he could see also her inner strength and the struggle for wisdom. He regarded the fineness of her features, the red–gold hair, the startling eyes, then made his decision.

Mindful of Aherne's hostility towards him, he spoke to Kay.

'It would appear that you do not disapprove of my invasion of Inisfail. If I knew that you would not interfere with my plans, I would help you in this quest you speak of.'

Aherne's eyes narrowed with distrust but Kay leaned forward eagerly.

'Will you give us back the Spear?'

Amergin nodded. A slight smile formed at the edges of his mouth.

'I have no use for it. Though it is a weapon of remarkable beauty, it is not meant to be wielded. But I offer you more than that. This ship is sailing to Inis Mor, the last freehold of the Firbolg nation. I will take you to my friend and ally, Cahal mac Umor, the High Chieftain of Dun Ealga. Between us we can provide you with whatever aid you need to continue your quest.'

Kay was overwhelmed. After the hardships involved in finding the first treasure, this offer was a gift of unexpected good fortune. A little warning sounded in her mind and cooled her inclination to shower him with gratitude.

'If you feel you owe us,' she said uneasily, 'it would be enough to return the Spear and set us free. Why are you offering more?'

'Because I want something in return,' the prince said.

Kay hesitated, uncertain whether or not she was prepared to bargain. But Aherne, who had smiled smugly at Kay's suspicion, lost her temper again. In a fit of rage she jumped from her chair and stood over Amergin.

'Are you not satisfied with taking my country? What more could you want from us?'

Amergin's eyes were dark with amusement but he was serious as he lifted his hand to grip her shoulder.

'You,' he said.

PART TWO

THE RISING QUEEN

JOURNEYS OF KAY AND AHERNE
BY GAEDIL SHIP TO INIS MOR - - - > - →
BY FIRBOLG CURRACH TO RIND TAMAIN ⟶
BY CHARIOT TO TAILLTIU ─ ∙ ─ ∙ ─ ∙ ─∙

N

62 miles

TORINIS

MAG MOYTURA

Sionann

Loch Uair

Loch Ribh

Uisnech

Taillтiu   Inber Colptha

Ath Luain

INIS MOR

Dun Ealga

INIS MEDON

Rind Tamain

Fidnach Bera

Cenn Baine

MAG
nADAR

River

Loch Ainnin

TEMAIR   Ben Edar

Dun Ailinne

River Slane

• Druim nAsail

Sliab Mis

Inber Scene

the land of inisfail
1500 b.c.

CHAPTER FOURTEEN

W HEN KAY WAS BROUGHT BEFORE
Cahal mac Umor, High Chieftain of Dun Ealga, she recognized
him immediately. For a moment she lost all sense of time and
place.

'Alan?'

He wore the rough attire of the Firbolg tribe, baggy
woollen trousers and cloak of raw cattle-hide. His hair was
cropped short, black in colour like his beard, giving him a stern
and rugged look. There was also a leanness that hinted of hardship as well as the proud air of one in command. But regardless
of the beard or any other difference, Kay stared into his strong
features and knew him.

As she recovered from her shock, she realized the truth. He
was undoubtedly the ancestor of the student who had befriended
her in her own time. Her voice echoed with warmth as she
greeted him.

'Your line will travel far, High Chieftain,' she said, startling
him as much by her friendly tone as by her words. 'From one
island to another and always noble.'

'Are you a Mage?' Cahal demanded with suspicion as he
found himself inexplicably liking her.

'Sort of,' she replied. 'But if you mean am I connected with
the Danaan Druids, the answer is no.'

Their friendship began with that answer.

He spent the day showing her Dun Ealga, a great stone fort on the western edge of the island of Inis Mor. Set upon the cliffs like a seabird's nest, it looked down over a perilous drop, a sheer side of rock that plunged into the endless sea. At the very edge of this precipice was Cahal's citadel, a tall square tower protected at its back by the unscalable sea cliffs and facing outwards to three massive ramparts of stone. The first wall was the highest and thickest. It rose up with stolid grandeur, enclosing the Chieftain's citadel and a wide space for his guard. The second wall ranged further afield, covering a terraced space of lawn. Behind this wall was an army of jagged stones set together in fierce profusion. Cahal pointed to the deadly barrier with pride.

'Amergin of the Gaedil taught us how to build this. It's a method of fortification from his own land which cuts short a running attack of men or beasts.'

'He's a good ally,' was Kay's comment.

'A good *friend,*' Cahal said.

The third wall ranged further still as it protected a wide area that housed the small stone buildings of the tribe as well as their meagre livestock. Kay watched the women mould clay into pots. Others worked patches of garden with tools of stone and flint. Old men mended nets and tackle while the younger ones went out on the sea to fish.

Kay noted the pinched faces of the Firbolg children, the thin bodies of both men and women. They lived a hard life on this windy island, harvesting the treacherous ocean for food. But she could see also that they were an indomitable race, unbowed by their poverty, and quick to laughter. With black hair, dark eyes and a wiry grace, they had a harsh beauty of their own.

Cahal took Kay's arm when they reached the final rampart and they climbed up the wall to look out at Inis Mor. In sight of the western coast of Inisfail, it was a lime-bright island of granite and stone, without soil, without trees, without people.

'We live only in the forts,' Cahal told her. 'My own Dun Ealga is the largest but there are two more on this island and another on Inis Medon south of here. There are also tribes on the mainland across from us but they are prey to Danaan raids. If we could only feed their numbers I would bring them all to these islands, our last refuge.'

'Are the Danaans trying to wipe out your race?' asked Kay, thinking of the Formorians.

The High Chieftain's answer was short and bitter.

'No. They use us as slaves.'

A shudder of revulsion passed through Kay as she imagined this proud man bent under the yoke of slavery.

Cahal was looking across the green waves to where the dim outline of Inisfail rose up through the mists. His voice echoed with an old sadness.

'So long ago it was when the Firbolg ruled the mountains and forests of Inis Ealga, that noble island now named Inisfail. Nearly two thousand years. My mind pales at the notion. I have never known my homeland and yet like all my tribe I yearn to return to it. Living in sight of its bright shadow, we keep its memory alive in our songs and stories.'

'I take it the Tuatha De Danaan invaded your country,' Kay said.

Cahal nodded, his eyes dim with thought. 'When they first came into the land, shining like beings of light, my race were afraid to approach them. But Eochaid mac Erc, our High Chieftain and lawmaker, raised the Firbolg for war and met the invaders on the plain. The First Battle of Moytura. We were defeated but the conquerors were kind. Though Eochaid died in that battle, his wife Taillte married a Danaan lord to make peace amongst the tribes. She was beloved of both nations and was the foster-mother of the Danaan King Lug. In her honour Lug named the wide rath where the Danaan games are held "Tailltiu." And so it is called even now, despite all enmity.'

'So the Danaans weren't bad at first,' Kay said. 'But what happened? Why is it different now?'

Cahal shook his head as if bewildered.

'There were generations of peace, or so the ancient stories tell us. The Firbolg roamed the highlands while the Tuatha De Danaan settled the plains. But somehow they began to change. They grew disdainful of labour, became more cruel and warlike. They levied a tax upon my people. A human tax. Our sons to work in their fields and mines. Our daughters to serve in their great halls. We were powerless against them and had no choice but to render that onerous tribute. It has been a long time since the Danaan race put their own hands to work.

'Then a new people came to Inisfail, the tall sea-roving Formorians and we found stouthearted allies in our cause.' Cahal looked out at the sea that crashed against the shores of his island. His eyes flashed with admiration. 'A valiant race, the Formorians, furious lovers of freedom bred on the waves of the sea. At the Second Battle of Moytura we fought together against the Danaan overlords and the Formorians were above all others in courage and prowess.'

That's when the Formorians got the Spear, Kay thought to herself.

Cahal sighed heavily. 'But we were defeated in the end by the Danaan Druids and their arts of wizardry. The Firbolg race in its entirety was enslaved from that day forth. Some fled to the western wilds of the country to escape this fate. My own ancestors came to these islands which are now our last freehold. But we are always in the shadow of Danaan might.'

The High Chieftain looked with satisfaction at the three great walls of his fort, but when he turned to Kay his eyes were dark.

'It was the valorous Formorians who suffered the worst of fates. Mercilessly the Tuatha De Danaan hunted them down and slaughtered them like beasts. I have heard terrible tales of continued murder. Once they were masters of the sea in their great ships. Now they are naught but a pitiful handful, huddled on the northernmost isle of Inisfail.'

When Kay thought of Liag and her tribe and their huge effort to build a tower that would guide them to safety, her eyes filled unexpectedly.

'It's not right,' she murmured. 'I'm glad they're free at last.'

Her voice brought Cahal back to the present and he noticed her tears. His stern features softened.

'You have much compassion, Lady, but I do not wish to sadden you. The future of the conquered races in this land shines brightly now. Tonight we shall have a feast in celebration of that.'

Cahal talked of lighter things as they made their way back to his hall, but all the time Kay was thinking to herself that Aherne should have come on that walk with them.

Kay sighed as she thought of her young companion. The girl was wracked with her own torment, hiding from everyone in her chamber in Cahal's citadel. The voyage to Inis Mor had been a long and trying one as Aherne flew from tantrums to tears till Kay's patience wore thin.

'Who are you fighting against?' she had demanded angrily of Aherne. 'Him or yourself? We don't have to accept his terms. We can do it without him. Why are you so upset?'

'Because I *want* to accept his terms!' Aherne had wailed, flinging her goblet at the cabin door. 'It is a madness and I cannot stop it. I love him and I cannot fight it.'

Kay relented then and drew the girl down beside her.

'I can't really help you with this, Aherne. I've never been in love and I don't know what it feels like. But whatever happens, don't let him force you into a decision you don't want to make. Do what's right for *you*, no matter how much you love him.'

'But I do not want to love him at all,' Aherne said, with pain and unhappiness. 'I cannot love my enemy.'

★   ★   ★

Cahal's feast began at sunset. The Firbolg of Dun Ealga and the Gaedil of Amergin's ship gathered on the level space within the second rampart. Bonfires filled the air with fiery sparks and the sweet smell of burning wood. Huge cauldrons were set on hot stones, bubbling with sea crabs, spiced fish, oysters and prawns. Nuts were roasted in bronze pans on the fire and wooden platters were passed from hand to hand, laden with figs and apples, goat's cheese and dark bread. A thick black ale flowed from deep vats and as soon as one was emptied another was brought to take its place.

The Gaedil raided their own ship's larder to bring meat to the feast. Pork, venison and beef turned on spits and dripped over the flames. And as well as the meat there were Gaedil sweetcakes and honey, and red and white wine.

A wild music accompanied the celebration. The Firbolg musicians beat drums of hide and clattered frenziedly on hollowed bones. The Gaedil chased their mad rhythms with the high trills of flutes and the stringed resonance of harps. In the red shadows of the fires, figures danced with abandon, shouting and laughing.

Kay sat with Cahal on a stone bench beneath the wall, watching the uproarious crowd. Though the Gaedil shone in their finery and jewels, it was the Firbolg who danced with the most riotous joy. Many were painted with yellow and purple dye, the luxuriant swirls defying their lack of adornment. They dressed alike, both men and women, in dark wool trousers and vests of hide. Their feet were wrapped in raw cowskin tied with string.

Beneath her cloak, Kay herself wore the dress of the islanders, and she had bound her hair in braids looped around her ears in the manner of the Firbolg women.

Cahal smiled at her with appreciation.

'You do me honour to take our ways.'

'Yours is an honourable tribe,' Kay replied.

She was happy in his company and as they talked together, their heads bowed towards each other in the closeness of friendship.

When Amergin joined them he looked from one to the other with an inquisitive smile. Cahal jumped to his feet and embraced the prince heartily.

'Have I thanked you for the fine food?'

Amergin laughed. 'The Firbolg must get used to eating well. They have had thin fish enough in their lifetime.'

'You are right there,' Cahal said, patting his stomach happily. 'What is freedom compared to a full belly? I would have been hard-pressed if you had offered me a choice instead of both.' Aware that he was stating a half-truth, he added with a quick laugh, 'I would sell my kingdom for that white meat.'

'No need, no need!' Amergin cried and he raced to catch a platter of pork before it made its rounds. He bowed before

Cahal and offered him the lot. 'I have some authority over my own,' he said lightly.

'You would want to,' said Cahal. 'They are a mad bunch, your Gaedil. The women as bad as the men. They have emptied three of my ale vats already.'

Kay laughed at the antics of the two and yet she couldn't help thinking that she would enjoy herself more if only Aherne would join them. But the girl had refused to attend the feast.

Amergin was still bantering with Cahal when he suddenly became distracted. Kay followed his look and saw Aherne standing near the musicians.

She wore the shining raiment of the Gaedil, a gown of amaranthine sewn with discs of gold. The discs sparkled like eyes when she moved and she was swaying with lithe grace in time to the music. Her features were lost in the wild sound.

Kay looked at her closely. Something was odd. The girl's beauty was more striking than usual. Her fiery hair, so closely shorn but a while ago, now rippled on her shoulders in red-gold curls. And she seemed taller somehow. Kay sat up as the realization struck her. Some power was affecting Aherne. And Kay, too, was feeling incredibly light and elated. This had happened on Torinis when the Spear was found. Another treasure was nearby!

Kay's thoughts were interrupted as Amergin leaned towards her eagerly.

'Does she like to dance?' he asked, nodding his head towards Aherne.

Kay gave him a noncommittal smile.

'Why don't you find out?'

Amergin's lips tightened. 'She will probably knock me over like the Formorian guard. However,' he said with a grin, 'it is worth the risk.'

Cahal and Kay watched with amusement as the Prince of the Gaedil stepped gingerly towards the girl. The firm set of his shoulders, the anxious tilt of his head, showed his wary resolve.

'Lady, do you dance?' he asked, proffering his hand to Aherne. His voice was casual but his brown eyes flashed with hope.

Aherne hesitated. The music was racing through her blood like a dark tide. She loved to dance. And she loved the man who bowed gracefully before her. The impassioned sound was rising to a crescendo, carrying with it her thoughts and desires. But she did not feel lost. A nameless power was stirring within her. She felt as if she could stride up a mountain, stretch out her arm and pluck the stars from the sky.

She tossed her red-gold hair and placed her hand in his.

'Come dance with me!'

Chapter Fifteen

Both Kay and Cahal smiled as the two dancers joined the swirling crowd. The High Chieftan looked thoughtful.

'Amergin has told me the terms he offers you and it seems the girl has a liking for him. He is wise for one so young. A Danaan marriage could lead to a peaceful settlement of the land.'

'I think it's more than politics,' Kay said with a grin, then she grew serious as she remembered the treasure. 'Are *you* willing to help us?'

Cahal frowned before answering. 'In this one short day I have met and liked you, Kay. But I know the nature of your quest from speaking with Amergin and as it is for the good of the Danaan race, I cannot help you. To be true to my people, I could not further the aims of my enemy.'

'The quest won't affect what you and Amergin are doing. I'm sure of it,' she said urgently. 'The Gaedil will rule Inisfail and your people will be set free. As far as I'm concerned,' she added with a shrug, 'it's already history.'

Cahal raised his eyebrows but his voice was firm.

'I know you are a Mage but you must understand that I cannot accept your word. The invasion has yet to take place and I must guard its outcome. The lives and dreams of my tribe depend upon it.'

'But I just told you,' Kay said, exasperated. 'The invasion will take place and it will succeed. Nothing can change that. Your future is my past and . . .' She could see that he wasn't convinced though she sensed also that he wanted to believe her. His duty simply would not allow him. He obviously needed more solid proof. 'Cahal,' she said quietly, 'I can *show* you if you'll let me. I can show you my knowledge.'

He stared at her uncertainly and then nodded his agreement.

Kay didn't stop to choose her images. She simply thought of her own time and sent the pictures into Cahal's mind. The High Chieftain's face showed his astonishment as he caught glimpses of cities and highways, cars and airplanes, modern buildings and fashions. With sudden inspiration, Kay sent him a memory of herself, sitting in her apartment and translating one of her books. She drew him closer and had him read through her eyes, the pages that told of the Gaedil invasion. Then she ended the images and waited for his reaction.

Cahal's face was white. He looked around him shakily to get his bearings. The glare of the bonfires and the noise of the celebration reassured him, but his eyes still echoed confusion and fear. He spoke in an accusing tone.

'How do I know this was not a trick of enchantment?'

Kay's anger was instant.

'What a rotten thing to say! I've been telling you the truth and now I've shown it to you and you're still calling me a liar. If I wanted to use "enchantment" I could just as well use it to force you into helping me. But I happen to consider you a friend though the feeling obviously isn't mutual. I wouldn't force you even if I could and I probably could, come to think of it,' she finished with a huff.

It was Kay's tirade that convinced Cahal in the end. He put more store in his own judgement of character than in any magical power or special knowledge. He could see quite clearly that she was hurt by his disbelief.

'Forgive me,' he said quietly and he lifted her hand to his lips. 'I have spent my life as a soldier and it has left me lacking in trust and courtesy.'

'That's all right,' she replied, smiling shyly at his gesture. 'So does that mean you'll help me?'

'It does indeed,' Cahal said with a laugh. 'But what kind of help do you need?'

Kay spoke eagerly. 'The quest is for ancient treasures. We have the Spear which we found on Torinis. The Sword is in the hands of the Danaan Druids. The Stone is the most powerful one and I think will be found last. That leaves the Cauldron. I can't say how I know it but I'm certain, Cahal, that it's here on your island. But where should I look for it?'

The High Chieftain had been listening with quiet amazement, but as soon as Kay mentioned the Cauldron he was suddenly intent.

'Perhaps I *can* help you,' he said. 'When I was a boy I used to play on the cliffs, hunting for gulls' nests. There was a cave within the rocks. And in that cave was a deep pool, dark and sinister with water cold as the grave. It was only a child's name but what child named it I cannot say. All of us called it the Cauldron Pool.'

'That must be it!' Kay cried. She jumped up and pulled at Cahal's arm. 'Show me where it is. I must see it!'

In her eagerness and excitement, Kay didn't think about the darkness of the night or about Aherne who was still dancing around the bonfires. It was as if the treasure were drawing her inexorably to itself.

Cahal was caught up in Kay's zeal and after his earlier distrust he felt bound to support her.

They left the feast and the sheltering walls of Dun Ealga and made their way down the wind-swept cliffs. The ocean roared with haunting sound. Illumined by moonlight, the waves struck the coast with white crests of foam. Ever mindful of the swirling abyss below, Kay and Cahal picked their way over the treacherous rock.

Hand clasped in Cahal's, Kay was exhilarated by the descent into darkness and sound. It was a world of cliff and wind and water, dark dripping stone and spuming sea. The heady salt air and the tearing winds made her dizzy with the vigour of nature. She now understood the ingenuity of the Firbolg boots and she was glad she was wearing them. The wrappings were not only thick enough to stop the sharp ground from cutting her, but they shifted with the movements of her feet and allowed her to grasp toeholds and narrow ledges.

Further down amongst the rocks was a spot where the cliffs turned inward like a maw of craggy teeth. The great cave swallowed the sea waves in furious gulps and spewed them out again in bursts of spray.

'The pool is in there,' Cahal shouted over the roar of the water.

Kay wiped the salty dampness from her face and followed behind him. It was like walking into a giant conch. The wind rushed through the cavern with loud sighs. The two trod a high ledge that kept them above water, then crawled beneath a roof of stony icicles into the heart of the cave. There was the pool, sunk deeply in the rocks, fed by the churning sea below. The water was black as night, surging and slapping with an ominous sound.

Kay knelt at the edge of the pool and peered into its dark face.

I wish I could swim, she thought with a little moan, but she was already unwrapping her boots.

'You are not going in there,' Cahal stated flatly.

'I have to,' Kay said in a low voice. 'I'm sure the treasure is under the water. And whether I like it or not . . .'

The High Chieftain took hold of her arm and it wasn't a gentle touch.

'I command you to stay. This land is under my law. You must obey me. I swam here as a child and I have promised to aid you. *I* shall dive for the treasure.'

His eyes were hard. Kay could see the firm set of his jaw beneath his beard. She knew there was no point in arguing and she considered commanding him in turn with the power of her mind. But her respect for him was too great. She accepted his offer and smiled at him with sudden humour.

'I hope you're not putting the same terms on your aid as Amergin did.'

His dark eyes lit up with laughter.

'Have you been looking into my mind again, Mage?' He brushed her face lightly with his fingers. 'No, I am not as arrogant as that young pup.'

They both laughed and Kay looked at him with fond concern.

'Think of me as you swim,' she said seriously. 'I can make it easier for you.'

'I shall think of you,' he agreed with a wink.

Cahal stripped off his clothes and crouched at the rim of the pool. His broad back was a white shadow against the dark water. With a sleek swift movement he made his dive.

Kay closed her eyes and concentrated on Cahal. He *was* thinking of her. She joined easily with his mind, all the images welling up to drown her also. Black water, fierce cold, and the sickening motion of the pool's current.

He swooned as the water sucked him down.

'Steady, my friend,' she whispered as she sent him images of the Cauldron she could sense beneath him.

It was on a ledge submerged within the pool, not too far below him. But he was running out of breath. Kay could feel his suffocation. She urged him on, aware that he had grasped the rim of the Cauldron. He was tugging at it wildly to loose it from its perch. Kay sent him images of the sky and the expanse of air to still his heaving lungs. At last the Cauldron was free. But Cahal flailed in panic as the weight of it pulled him down.

Kay herself began to panic. Which was more important? Cahal or the quest? She couldn't hold both him and the Cauldron. She had to choose. Her instinct rose to help her. She couldn't let a friend die for the sake of a thing, no matter its importance. She sent him images of the Cauldron falling, but he resisted her commands. Still he held onto it and deeper he sank.

'No, Cahal!' she cried out loud, bending over the deathly pool.

She knew he couldn't reach the surface with the Cauldron. He would drown in his desire to help her.

Kay's decision was immediate. She threw off her cloak and plunged into the pool. As she felt herself sinking into the depths, a fleeting thought crossed her mind. This is how it must have been for Aherne when she jumped across the Tower of Conaing. Fear was forgotten in the need to save a friend. Kay didn't think about the fact that she couldn't swim. Her mind was bent on finding Cahal. And even as she struggled in the cold and dark, she felt the power of the Cauldron surge towards her.

'To me! To me!' she commanded fiercely, using the new power it had given her itself.

The Cauldron rose to meet her, carrying Cahal in its wake. Before they knew what had happened, the two broke the surface of the pool with the treasure between them.

Choking and spluttering, they climbed out of the water.

'I ordered you not to go in!' Cahal said furiously, as soon as his throat was clear.

'And I was ordering you to drop the Cauldron,' Kay said in the same tone. 'You knew I was and you still held onto it!'

'That was my decision!' he shouted. 'I am the law on this island.'

'Stuff your law!' Kay shouted back. 'You don't make decisions for me. I wasn't going to let you die.'

'You could have died yourself!' was his loud reply.

Face to furious face both realized in that moment the reason for their rage. Each was thoroughly undone by the thought of the other's death. As they acknowledged that truth with sudden silence, humour broke through their anger.

'Put your clothes on,' Kay said, starting to laugh. 'I can't argue with you standing there like that.'

Cahal let out a roar of laughter and dressed quickly in the cold. He reached for Kay's cloak and as he wrapped it around her, he pulled her to him in a long embrace. Then he heaved the Cauldron onto his back.

'To my hall, fair adventurer,' he said with a grin. 'We have done a good night's work and deserve hot punch.'

They were sitting together in the High Chieftain's chamber when Aherne and Amergin found them. Kay had changed into dry clothing and was combing out her hair before the fire. Cahal had fetched a plate of Gaedil pastries and was eating them one after the other, occasionally popping a tidbit into Kay's mouth as well. They had cups of spiced wine warmed over the hearth, and their voices murmured in laughter and talk.

'Ah, a private celebration!' Amergin said with a mischievous grin.

Kay stared back at him without blinking and then smiled at Aherne. The younger girl was holding Amergin's hand and the two looked flushed and happy.

'It's a night for celebrating all right,' Kay said. 'We've found another treasure.'

'What?' cried Aherne with a mixture of joy and regret. 'Without me?'

Kay looked amused. 'Don't worry the next one *you* can take alone.'

But Aherne wasn't listening. She had run over to the Cauldron where it stood beside the Spear, and was exclaiming over its beauty. The deep bowl was of ivory, smooth and perfect like a pearl, and the diamond rim glittered like the blood of a star.

'I should have known it was near,' Aherne said softly. 'Just like the Spear on Torinis, I have felt its power all day.'

'Me too,' Kay nodded, her eyes shining.

'Strange women we have here,' Amergin commented to Cahal as he poured himself a cup of wine. He poured one for Aherne and handed it to her with a quizzical smile.

They drew up chairs beside Kay and Cahal and the four sat together before the hearth.

'Strange women indeed,' Cahal said after a while. He was tugging at his beard as he stared into the flames. 'While we plot war, they are busy with something far greater.'

A shadow crossed Amergin's face. He glanced anxiously at Aherne.

'For this one night only,' he said in a low urgent plea, 'let us steal from time and forget what lies ahead. There is no war. There is no quest. Only four friends, good wine and a cheerful fire.'

The four looked at each other, aware of the bittersweet nature of the moment. Though the strength of youth and friendship was on their side, all were entangled in the web of a conflicting world. But here was a moment of freedom if they chose to take it, a quiet time in the midst of the storm.

'A game,' Aherne suggested playfully. 'Let each name what the other loves most. And I do not mean persons,' she added hastily to the quick laughter of the others.

'I shall guess for you,' Cahal said, courteously saving her from embarrassment. 'The Firbolg are renowned for their love and skill of dance, but you are the finest dancer I have ever seen. You moved as if the music were a secret language that you speak. I believe you have an inner sense of beauty. Art and especially music is what you hold dearest.'

Aherne beamed with pleasure and bowed her head in assent.

'You must name his now,' Amergin said, catching the spirit of the game.

Aherne looked seriously at the High Chieftain for the first time. She saw the strength of his features, the wisdom and kindness in his eyes. She looked around his chamber, an austere and spartan room, stone wall rising sternly to stone roof with the occasional weapon hanging in state. A soldier's chamber, but he did not seem like a man of war. Only Kay saw the dawning knowledge in Aherne's eyes and the remorse that came with it.

'You are a man of duty,' Aherne said slowly. 'You cherish order above all things. The order of just rule and the good of your people.'

Cahal was taken aback, not expecting such a judgement from a Danaan girl but he replied gravely that what she said was true.

'I am sorry,' she whispered to him. 'We have done you much wrong.'

He lifted his hand and smiled gently at her.

'Within this room and on this night, all is well.'

'Clever Mage,' Amergin said to Kay with a lively grin. 'You must name my preference.'

'I'd easily win if I said spirited women were your first love,' Kay said dryly and the others laughed, though Aherne blushed as well. 'But I'll try to come up with your second love.'

She paused as she looked at the bright face of the Gaedil prince. The others had used their particular powers of observation and Kay decided she could use hers. Lightly she touched the edges of his mind as a bather dabbles in the shallows of the sea. A maze of images greeted her: machines of war and tools of trade; the plans and designs for intricate structures; buildings and ships, aqueducts and tombs. It went on and on. His mind was a clutter, a magpie's nest of marvellous objects and the details of their construction. Kay smiled with humour and respect.

'You're more than a leader,' she said at last. 'My guess is that you rule by birth not choice. You'd much rather tinker around with what I call technology. You love machines and things that have practical uses and all the skills that go with them. The work of a carpenter, a sailor, a soldier, a builder, a weaver, a potter . . .'

Amergin's eyes grew bigger as her list went on, naming all the things which had caught his interest since childhood. Then he threw up his hands to finish her list with his own addition.

'Do not forget the skill of a Mage, especially one who has the power to read minds.'

'Oh, that is cheating, is it not?' Aherne cried and they roared with laughter as Kay protested.

'Fair lady, I shall give as good as I got,' Amergin stated. 'My years of "unwilling" rule have at least taught me how to read any man or woman.'

He gave her a long look of appraisal, noting the high colour in her face. The grey eyes shone in that little company far brighter than he had seen them shine since he had met her. He spoke with quiet confidence.

'Because you are a Mage, it would be easy to say that you are a seeker of knowledge who yearns to know the meaning and purpose of your power. But my guess for you goes beyond that. The life of a seeker is a solitary one, wandering over lonely peaks to find the wisdom of the stars. Laughter comes too easily to your lips to make you a contented exile. I say that against the solitude of your power you cherish friendship above all things.'

The others were silent when he finished speaking. Amergin was already holding Aherne's hand and she in turn took Cahal's as the High Chieftain reached out for Kay. Though tears clouded her eyes, a slow smile came across Kay's face. Then she nodded in surrender and leaned forward to take Amergin's hand. The game was over. The circle was complete.

Chapter Sixteen

THE COUNCIL OF WAR WAS HELD
in the main hall of Cahal's citadel where the great windows
looked west over the luminous sea. Another ship had reached
the island late that afternoon, bearing Amergin's brothers, Eber
and Eremon, with their commanders. The Gaedil filled the hall,
a noisy laughing company. The young men and women were
dressed in battle array with bronze swords at their waists, copper
spears in their hands, and great shields engraved with the sign
of the boar. Rich mantles fell from proud shoulders and golden
torcs gleamed at their throats. With the nut-brown skin of
their sunny homeland and eyes flashing with anticipation, they
looked a bright and lively people.

The Firbolg leaders were also present; Conor mac Umor,
Cahal's uncle, from the fortress of Inis Medon, and the chieftains of the mainland tribes of Cenn Baine, Fidnach Bera, Rind
Tamain, Mag nAdar and Druim nAsail. All older men, grey-
haired and bearded, they had sworn allegiance to Cahal's father
and now answered the call of his son as High Chieftain. They
stood stolidly in their rough trousers and cloaks of hide, stone
axes leaning heavily on their shoulders and flint daggers tucked
into their belts. They looked distrustfully at the smooth faces
and rich clothing of the Gaedil, but the friendship of Cahal and
Amergin was obvious and contagious. Slowly the commanders

of both races met and mingled. When the Council was called to order, all gathered together at the table which held a map of Inisfail.

In a room above the great hall, Kay and Aherne were watching the Council though their viewing went undetected.

Kay had argued long and loudly with Cahal that she needed to know his plans for the good of the quest. But despite her insistence that she wouldn't interfere with the invasion, the High Chieftain had remained adamant.

'I assisted you in finding the treasure,' he had stated with finality. 'What you ask now is impossible. I will not endanger my people by allowing you to hear the battle plan.'

Frustrated and unhappy, Kay had returned to her chambers and paced the floor moodily.

'I'm sure the quest and the invasion are mixed up together,' she said to Aherne. 'We've got to know what's happening! The stories didn't tell me everything.'

Aherne shook her head angrily. 'I do not want to hear what they have in store for Inisfail.'

Kay stopped pacing to put her hands on the girl's shoulders.

'I understand how you feel, but if the quest is to help your people then the more we know, the better.'

It was Aherne who came up with the suggestion that Kay use her power to spy on the Council.

'Why didn't I think of that myself?" Kay cried, giving her a hug.

The two crept into the small storeroom above the hall and sat cross-legged on the floor. Kay held Aherne's hand.

'Remember,' she whispered. 'We need to know this for the quest. Try to be strong no matter what you see or hear.'

Kay joined her mind with Aherne's even as she reached out for Cahal and Amergin below. As the four were bound in friendship the link was easy, though Kay cloaked what she was doing from the two men themselves. She didn't like doing it without their consent but she felt it was necessary. Once she had joined their minds, it was as if she and Aherne were in the hall with the others.

Amergin and Cahal stood together at the table as the commanders leaned over a roll of painted silk that displayed the land of Inisfail. A silence settled over the gathering as Amergin spoke with calm command.

'I, Prince of the Gaedil, have drawn up the battle plan with the help of my ally, Cahal, High Chieftain of the Firbolg tribes. We shall give you your orders now and you will position your armies and fleets accordingly.'

He tapped the map with authority.

'The Gaedil invasion of Inisfail begins from three points— the southwest, southeast and northeast. Eber, you will land your fleet at Inber Scene and march north to Sliab Mis to meet with Conor of the Firbolg and one hundred of his men. They will guide you across the southern lands and you will take every Danaan fort in your path till you march on Temair.'

Eber gave his assent with a gruff nod. Five years older than his brother, his features were similar to Amergin's but his look was harder and far less pleasant. There was no laughter or mischief in this son of Milidh, a serious, phlegmatic and single-minded man.

Seeing him in her mind, Aherne shuddered in the store-room above. She had no doubt that Eber would carry out his duty with thorough and brutal resolve. She was already mourning the fate of her people at his hands and she could only listen with helpless grief as the orders continued.

'Eremon, your fleet has already reached Alba and is well hidden? Good. I will report later on the false information we have fed the Danaan Druids but you must be wary of their spies. Inber Colptha is your landing point, brother. The most powerful of the Danaan forts are in this sector. You will march west to take the sacred centre of the Brugh na Boinne and the mighty raths of the Boann Valley. You have a small area to capture before you march on Temair but the fighting will be long and fierce as this is the heart of Danaan country. The rest of us will be moving towards you to reach Temair and we will send reinforcements if they are needed.'

Eremon tossed his head as he acknowledged his instructions. The eldest of Amergin's brothers and a veteran warrior, he gladly accepted the main thrust of the invasion. From countless campaigns he knew he was the man most suited for the task.

'As for myself,' Amergin said, smiling slightly. 'I shall land in the southeast at Inber Slaine and march north to take Dun Ailinne and the smaller hill forts around. It is my desire to reach Temair as soon as possible. Since the kingdom is to be mine, I must lead the attack on its royal centre.'

The Gaedil commanders expressed their assent to the plans and Amergin called on Cahal to give the Firbolg their orders.

'My blood kin,' Cahal said warmly to the chieftains. 'The Gaedil lead this conquest as it is their force which will ensure its success. But as you know they have offered us lands and freedom if we support their sovereignty. It is important that we play our part in what they are about to do. Except for Conor who will join Eber's army, you will all march with me. Have you distributed the Gaedil weapons among your warriors? Are your women ready with chariots and supplies? Well done. We will cross the country together, following always the Eisgir Riada, those hills which were once our own and will be so again. We will secure the middle of Inisfail like a fine belt strapped around our waists. Then we too shall march on Temair for the last battle. There is no doubt that as the land is torn asunder the Tuatha De Danaan will retreat to their greatest stronghold. When Temair falls, the conquest will be complete.'

Cahal allowed a moment's silence as all pondered the battle plan. The map of Inisfail lay before them and the gleam of victory beckoned like a torch.

Amergin cleared his throat and finished the presentation.

'My spies have been active within the royal circles of the Danaan tribe. The prophetic powers of the Druids have made them aware of the coming invasion. Though they do not know who we are or how great our force will be, they have armed their raths and called hostings of warriors. In the face of this, we have managed to delude them into believing that the conquest will not take place till several weeks hence. They will therefore be caught off guard by our sudden and earlier arrival. Any questions?'

Eremon was the first to speak, his voice calm and his gaze steady as he addressed Amergin.

'You have neglected the north, young brother. Beware the weak link in any strategy. I know it is not greatly populated but I see a Danaan cashel marked on this map and is there not another race in Inisfail, one who lives on some northern island?'

Amergin bowed his respect to Eremon but shook his head.

'You refer to the Formorians whom I had planned to take as allies. They would have secured the north but that is no longer necessary. The Danaan fort of Grianan Ailech was laid waste by the Formorians themselves who have since under-taken an exodus from Inisfail. We need not concern ourselves with the north till we come to settle it.'

'Your information is certain?' asked Eremon quietly.

'Yes,' Amergin replied.

In the room above, Kay smiled wryly to herself. The prince had used her information to streamline his plans. For all his light-heartedness, he was a quick and effective leader of war.

While Amergin and Eremon were speaking, the Firbolg chieftains had drawn aside to confer among themselves. They had not included Cahal and they looked uncomfortable when they met his eyes. It was Conor who spoke up and his tone was apologetic.

'We have a question, High Chieftain, but we would prefer to ask it of you alone.'

Cahal's frown was stern. 'There can be no discussions without our allies. Ask it here.'

Conor's embarrassment was evident but he plunged ahead.

'We mean no offence but we cannot help but ask. For the past year Amergin of the Gaedil has lived amongst us and we know of the bonding between you and him. This we trust, and his promise that the highlands and mountains of Inisfail will be returned to the Firbolg nation. But now his brothers have come to join the invasion and as they are older they take rightful precedence over him. How can we know that they will honour his promises when they too are kings in Inisfail?'

Cahal's face flushed with anger as did Eber's, but Eremon remained aloof while Amergin smiled.

'That question is easily answered,' Amergin said, raising his hand to cut off Cahal's protest. 'And no insult is taken. I will tell you why I have come into Inisfail and it will end your doubts.

'I am the youngest of eight sons of Milidh. In our home-land each of us holds a princedom under the High Kingship of our father. My own land of late has fallen into ruin. Floods, poor harvest and the death of the great mine of my chief city,

Los Millares, are but some of the misfortunes that have plagued my people. No effort of my own nor aid from my brothers has been able to overcome these disasters. I came to understand, then, that the gods wished me to seek a new country.

'My brothers Eber and Eremon are here to support me with their skills and troops. They will be returning to their own kingdoms when the conquest is over. It is my people and myself only who will settle in Inisfail. You can rest assured. I alone will be King and my promises will be met.'

The tension in the hall faded and even Eber managed a brief smile as the Firbolg chieftains cheered loudly.

Amergin and Cahal smiled at each other and when order was restored the prince concluded the Council.

'You have your instructions. Each of you will return now to your fleets and homes and see to the last of your preparations. The invasion begins three days hence at sunset. When we meet again, it will be at the victory feast in Temair.'

As the Council ended, Kay broke her concentration and looked at Aherne. The girl's face was ashen and her eyes sick with despair.

'My people are doomed,' she moaned.

Kay gripped Aherne's hands with urgent sympathy.

'I know it's hard and I'm sorry you had to hear that but don't give up yet, Aherne. We've still got the quest.'

Kay herself was thinking hard. What was the significance of all she had heard? She sensed a pattern taking shape and there was something important she had to grasp. The invasion would take place in three days. Surely that meant the quest must be completed by then. But how? And why?

'Does three days from now mean anything special to you?' she asked Aherne abruptly.

Aherne looked hurt and angry at the question.

'As we have just heard, the invasion of my country . . .' She stopped suddenly, her mouth still open. 'The feast of Lugnasad is three days away! And the games of Tailltiu!'

Kay trembled with excitement. 'Where the Druids are raising up the Sword! I knew it! The quest and the invasion are tied together somehow. This can't be just a coincidence. We're on the right path and moving closer all the time!'

With a jubilant cry, Kay jumped up and ran out of the storeroom and down to the hall.

Cahal and Amergin were sitting at the table, still talking over the map of Inisfail. Both looked tired but triumphant at the success of the Council and they smiled easily at Kay as she hurried towards them.

'You said you'd help us on the quest,' Kay said eagerly to the men. 'Aherne and I must reach Tailltiu in less than three days.'

Cahal's face looked like thunder and Kay knew he was about to accuse her of spying. She rushed her words ahead of him.

'I'm not interested in what you're doing, Cahal. Your games of war mean nothing to me. I'm after the third treasure, the Sword which the Druids are bringing to Tailltiu on the feast of Lugnasad. That takes place three days from now and we must get there before it starts.'

Cahal could hear the truth in her voice but he was alarmed by the coincidence of time involved.

'I cannot let you go,' he said flatly. Amergin nodded in agreement.

'Why not?' she demanded.

The two men frowned at each other. They couldn't state their reasons without giving away their plans.

'You promised to help us,' Kay pleaded.

The men looked confused and unsettled, but Kay could sense that their decision was firm. She was coming to the unwilling conclusion that she would have to force them with her power, when Aherne's voice rang out through the hall.

The girl stood with her green cloak wrapped around her and her face was fierce as she glared at Amergin.

'You offered me a pact. Your aid in return for my person. I call you to those terms now even as I accept them. You must help us reach Tailltiu to find the Sword.'

Cahal's eyes narrowed. He didn't like what was unfolding but he knew the decision rested with the prince. As leader of the invasion, Amergin had the last say.

The prince in turn was angrily aware that he had been caught in his own trap. By word of honour he couldn't withdraw his pact. Nor did he really want to.

'You can sail with me,' he said finally, though his voice sounded curt. 'I intend to anchor at Inber Slaine and I will give you horses to ride north to Tailltiu.'

But Cahal shook his head. 'If you are going to allow this, Amergin,' he said heavily, 'they may as well take the shorter route. They can reach the mainland tomorrow in a Firbolg boat and cross Inisfail from Rind Tamain. If we supply them with horse and chariot, their journey should take no more than two days at full speed.'

'That's what we'll do then,' Kay said with a satisfied nod. She smiled kindly at the discomfiture of the men. 'You won't be sorry, friends. I promise you.'

When the girls left, Cahal slapped the table. 'We must be mad!' he said. 'For all that I trust them, this is a dangerous move.'

Amergin sighed and shrugged his shoulders. 'I was caught in my own designs . . . but you don't think two women could affect a war?'

Cahal gave him a look that was hardly reassuring.

'They have already affected the leaders of the war, have they not?'

In their own chambers, Kay spoke unhappily to Aherne.

'I don't like it. That wasn't a free decision on your part. You're sacrificing yourself for the quest.'

'I accept that,' Aherne said in a hard and bitter voice. 'It is no longer a question of loving or hating him. No longer a question of my feelings at all. The doom of my people draws near and the quest is our only hope. I am prepared to do anything to find the last treasures.'

Chapter Seventeen

Two farewells were said that day before Kay and Aherne left for the mainland and both were marked by the sorrow of parting love.

Kay walked with Cahal along the high cliffs of Inis Mor, her arm resting on his in quiet intimacy. Seagulls and cormorants glided on the currents of air, their sad cries mingling with the roar of the sea below. Just beyond rose the stone walls of Dun Ealga, dark and impressive against the grey sky.

Cahal looked upon his fortress with a cold eye.

'After the conquest we shall abandon the dun and this island of stone. It was a refuge not a home. The Firbolg have never forgotten the warm woodlands and lofty mountains of our ancestors and we have ever yearned to return to them.'

He gazed out at the interminable expanse of water and his eyes no longer saw it.

'I will build a fort of fine timber with ramparts of earth and wood, and it will ring with the song of the birds of the forest. Music and poetry will resound in my hall. My tables will be laden with meat and fruit. And there will be hunting and feasting and laughter.'

He looked at Kay, hope shining in his dark eyes.

'Once that was all I dreamed of, but now I would have more.'

Kay remained silent, trying to ignore his plea till Cahal was driven to state it outright.

'Lady, if you would grace my hall I would be a happy man.'

Kay's eyes were sad and so too was her smile as she looked into the proud face of the High Chieftain.

'I didn't want you to say it, Cahal. You're only making it harder for both of us. What you're asking is impossible. I can't stay with you any more than you could come with me. I don't belong here. We've met for this short time only.'

He did not bother to hide his grief as he laid his hands on her shoulders.

'You see the future. Will we meet again?'

Kay fought against the hurt that was threatening to overwhelm her, but she knew inside what her answer had to be.

'No, Cahal. We won't meet again in Inisfail.'

The High Chieftain stood back from her, his face working with emotion as he struggled to accept her words. He stooped to the ground and picked up a stone, flinging it furiously over the cliff. It plummeted downwards into the blind and unfeeling ocean.

When he spoke again, his tone was one of finality and defeat.

'I dropped a stone into the sea and it was the stone of my heart.'

The parting of Aherne and Amergin was not as quiet, for the two shielded their sorrow with enmity and bad temper. He found her on the stony shore where she waited for Kay by the small boat that would take her from the island. She wore Firbolg clothes and her cloak was wrapped tightly around her in defence against the wind and her own emotions.

'By our friendship, at least, you could have bidden me farewell,' Amergin said angrily.

His temper hid his relief that she was still here. He had been aboard his ship, consulting with his commanders, and returned to Dun Ealga to find her chambers empty.

'I have nothing to say to you,' Aherne stated coldly.

But inside her a battle was raging. Two images, one dark, one light, clamoured in her mind as she stared into his face: the Council of War and Amergin plotting the invasion of her country with a cool eye and a triumphant voice; and against that, the bonfires of Dun Ealga, wild music and a starry night, and his arms around her as they danced together.

Amergin saw her confusion and reached out for her blindly. She pushed him away with anger and fear.

'You are my enemy!' she shouted.

Like her, he was explosive, tempestuous, lost. That he could do nothing to change what divided them made him rage all the more. But though he wanted her to love him willingly, he intended to claim her regardless.

'You accepted the pact,' he said, bitterness making him hard. 'You know the terms. After the conquest, I shall come for you.'

He turned on his heels and strode away, leaving her speechless with fury. She recovered enough to pick up a stone and hurl it after him, but her agitation caused her to throw wildly and miss. That infuriated her all the more and she screamed with frustration.

Aherne heard her own voice echoing its torment on the wind.

'Farewell, my love,' she whispered as the tears fell.

It was a silent crossing from Inis Mor to the mainland. Kay and Aherne huddled together in the small boat, each lost in her own sad thoughts. The Firbolg currach flew over the heavy waves like a seabird. Made of hide and wood, it was a supple craft but open to the sea spray and the wind. As the time passed in cold wet monotony and heaving discomfort, the girls forgot their personal miseries. When at last they reached the shores of Inisfail, they yearned only for warmth and the firmness of land.

The boatmen led them into the Firbolg village of Rind Tamain. It was a poor and hungry-looking settlement, crowded with small straw huts and smouldering fires. As they passed the dark-haired villagers, the girls lowered their eyes at the glances of hatred and anger. Their own fair colouring was the mark of the Danaan race and no friendship or greeting was offered to them. But they were well taken care of as the High Chieftain had commanded. They were brought into a little hut and, while their clothing dried, were given food and a hot brew that took the chill from their bones.

When the second currach arrived, carrying the Spear and the Cauldron, the treasures were placed in the chariot which was Cahal's last gift to them. While they were yoking the horses, a young woman approached them with fur blankets and provisions for their journey. They expected her to leave as silently as the others who had helped them, but she folded her arms and glared at Kay.

'I am Etair, daughter of the Chieftain of Rind Tamain.'

Kay looked with interest at the woman and wondered why she was vaguely familiar. Etair's features were strong and pretty though hardened by anger. A suspicion crept into Kay's mind and it was confirmed when the woman spoke bitterly.

'I have loved Cahal for many years and our fathers promised us in marriage when we were children. I did not force the betrothal knowing that Cahal had but one dream and one desire, the freedom of his people. But now as that freedom which should bring my happiness draws near, you have ruined all. I curse you for—'

'Don't,' Kay said quietly. 'It isn't necessary,' and she smiled suddenly as if a weight had been lifted from her heart.

Etair wasn't expecting that smile and she stared at Kay in confusion.

'He's yours,' Kay stated firmly. Then she repeated what she told Cahal the day she met him, 'And your line will be a long and noble one.'

Etair's face showed the conflict of her emotions. Joy mingled with uncertainty and distrust.

Kay shrugged impatiently. 'You must have heard I'm a Mage with whatever else you were told. I'm not lying to you. Why should I? I'm giving you good news not bad.'

Though still a little dazed, the woman nodded at last as she accepted what Kay said.

'Then I thank you for telling me this.' Etair paused, curiosity about her rival now rose as the threat diminished. 'But you love him also, do you not?'

'What difference does that make now?' Kay said sadly and she climbed into the chariot to end the conversation.

Aherne jumped in beside her and took up the reins. As they sped from the village, leaving Etair still staring after them, Aherne glanced at Kay.

'That was very generous of you. I would not have told her regardless of the truth.'

Kay laughed and sat down on the chariot bench as they rattled over the ground.

'It was really more for myself than her. If she doesn't marry him, I'll lose a promising friend in my own time.' She laughed again. The prospect of the aeons being so finely linked together made her feel light-headed. 'That's the trouble with travelling in time,' she added humorously. 'You can lose track of it so easily.'

'What *is* the difference in time for you, Kay?' Aherne asked. 'How far in the future do you belong?'

Kay looked at the hills that rolled along the horizon. They would be no different in her day, she mused.

'It's hard to say,' she answered at last. 'The books I read about your people were more legend than fact . . . but they did have some historical notes at the back. It seems to be debatable as to when your race ruled Inisfail or when the "sons of Milidh" came into the land. One of the notes suggested 1500 B.C. or thereabouts, though that wouldn't mean anything to you. What I should say,' and Kay was suddenly awed at the thought of it, 'over three thousand years lie between you and me.'

This was met with a stunned silence on Aherne's part as she directed her energy to keep control of the horses. With the reins in one hand and the goad in the other, she was handling the chariot with unconscious skill.

Kay admired the girl's prowess and rising confidence but she wasn't surprised. All the days of their adventuring and the power of the treasures had worked their effect. Aherne was no longer the pale and sickly child whom Kay had dragged from the bushes on her first night in Inisfail. Tall and strong limbed, she was a young and graceful woman with hair that fell like a stream of copper down her slim back.

'It's almost time,' Kay told herself, for the treasures were working on her also. As the power of her mind increased so too did her knowledge. She no longer depended solely on her instinct for the true. The pattern she had first glimpsed after the Council of War was now clear in her mind. She had finally seen the connection between the quest and the conquest. And she knew also the part that she and Aherne must play.

CHAPTER EIGHTEEN

THEY RODE LATE INTO THE evening, pressing onwards despite the onset of darkness. They had the breadth of Inisfail to cross and little time for such a journey. Aherne's knowledge of the land rose in her memory to guide them. They travelled for miles, the horses galloping with furious speed as if taking part in a chariot race.

'We will have to ford the River Sionnan,' Aherne shouted over the noise of the rattling carriage. 'I know a good place, Ath Luain, south of the wide lake of Loch Ribh.'

They called a halt after the wet crossing at the ford. The horses were flecked with foam from their arduous pace and Kay and Aherne were exhausted. Though the ford was shallow enough to take the chariot, the wheels kept sticking on the muddy bottom. The girls had to push from behind as the horses strained in front.

By the dark flow of the River Sionnan, they lit a fire and, after a quick supper, lay down to sleep.

Aherne pulled the Firbolg rug over her shoulders and grinned tiredly at Kay.

'We are "on the road" again as you would say, Kay.'

Kay smiled sleepily. 'And it's much easier with a chariot.'

'But what are we going to do in Tailltiu?' Aherne wanted to know.

'Tomorrow,' Kay murmured, drifting into sleep. 'Tomorrow I'll tell you.'

They woke before dawn and set off immediately, eating their breakfast of bread and dried figs as they drove. Mindful of the horses and the long day's journey ahead, Aherne kept the pace steady but comfortable. They travelled through the central lowlands, a mosaic of bog and grassland with brown mire in the hollows and high ridges of green. In the distance, ever present on the horizon, were the rolling hills of shadow-blue, fringed with dark patches of forest. The line of trees would bend in the wind like a troop of giant horsemen riding to the summit.

The girls were happy, sometimes singing, sometimes talking but also sharing the long companionable silences that only true friends can enjoy. They knew that this was but a brief spell of peace before the trials and dangers ahead, and they basked in the warm winds that blew their hair and the yellow sun that shone on their faces. Two friends in the green solitude of the countryside.

Now and then they came in sight of Danaan raths set on the slopes of hills and encircled by palisades of wood or stone. Aherne avoided them carefully.

'The hill fort of Uisnech lies just north of here,' Aherne said at one point, 'a great and royal residence of the Tuatha De Danaan.'

She grimaced sadly. That she had to evade her own people was a reminder of the coming invasion which she was bound to keep secret.

'We can't warn them,' Kay had replied vehemently to Aherne's suggestion. 'And it's not just a case of keeping trust with Cahal and Amergin. If we change what has to happen, the quest will be ruined.'

At midday they stopped between the lakes of Uair and Ainnin to let the horses graze a while before they set off again. By the time twilight brought its dim hush to the land, they had reached Odba, the territory which held the centres of Tailltiu and Temair.

Once more the girls camped down for the night, pleased with their timing and content that Tailltiu was a short distance away. They built their camp fire near the banks of a small river. As Aherne took out the last of their food she snorted with disgust at the dried fish flakes and hard bread.

'We need better than this after all our travelling,' she said, rummaging through their firewood to find a sharp stick.

Kay watched in silence as Aherne waded into the shallows of the river, standing knee deep and still in the cold black water. With a sudden pounce like a cat she jabbed downwards to spear a fine trout. She threw it on the riverbank and continued her efforts till their dinner was a feast of succulent roast fish.

'That was great,' Kay said as she licked her fingers. 'For someone without a memory you know a lot of things, don't you? How to dance, the geography of the land, chariot driving and now fishing. What more, I wonder?'

Aherne frowned and her green eyes clouded with confusion. 'I cannot say where the knowledge comes from. I do not remember learning these things but they are in my mind so I must have been taught them.'

Kay sighed. She knew what she had to do but she was worried about the effect it would have on her friend.

'Can you run a race?' Kay asked.

A flicker of fear crossed Aherne's face as she knew immediately what Kay meant.

'The Sword is the prize of the women's race at Tailltiu,' Kay said steadily. 'One of us has to run for it.'

'I thought we would steal it somehow,' Aherne said hopefully.

Kay shook her head. 'I think it's obvious that the treasures must be earned. We took the first together. I strove for the second. You should win the third.'

Aherne was unsettled. She could feel her mind heaving darkly. Something terrible loomed ahead. Dread rose within her and another emotion she couldn't name.

'But the Druids are holding up the Sword as the sovereignty of Inisfail,' she protested. 'Whoever wins it will be Queen and their pawn. That is not right. Even if the Rising Queen is dead—'

'Eriu is not dead,' Kay said flatly.

Aherne's face paled but her voice was stubborn.

'More so then, I cannot and will not take what is rightfully hers.'

Kay sighed heavily as she put more wood on the fire.

'You're very slow sometimes, Aherne. Your height now reaches mine and your hair is falling to your waist. Even as the treasures have restored your body they've been restoring your memory and your mind. But you're fighting it.'

Kay drew her hood over her face. In the shadow of the cowl only her grey eyes shone out at Aherne.

'Think, girl, why did the Druids call the Sentinels to kill Eriu?'

Something inside Aherne warned her not to answer, but Kay was waiting with intractable patience.

'Their visions revealed that the Rising Queen was a traitor,' Aherne said grudgingly.

'Why?' came Kay's relentless voice.

'Because of her love . . .' Aherne began to tremble. Her voice was a whisper, 'for the enemy king.'

Kay sensed her friend's turmoil, could see she was struggling against the knowledge she didn't want to face. Kay leaned forward to grasp Aherne's arms.

'It's time to remember. You can't avoid it any longer. With the strength of the treasures and with my help now, the truth can't hurt you. *What drove you into the forest in madness and despair?*'

Aherne couldn't move in Kay's grip. Her mind was spinning as memory rose to the surface like froth in a whirlpool. She stared into the cool grey eyes of the Mage and spoke in a dull tone.

'Wandering alone on the ramparts of Temair. My time is coming. I know that all is wrong. Banba, Fodla and those who came before. Too weak. Power and law in the hands of the Druids. Enemies everywhere, sullen and waiting to pounce. I know what I must do. Seek the help of the Goddess. I travel in secret to the Brugh na Boinne. Lie myself down on the wattles of wisdom. Cover my fear with the great bull hide. In the darkness, the bull-sleep comes to me. I see it. A new race in the land of Inisfail. I see it. The passing of the Danaan order. I see . . . I see . . .'

Tears streamed down Aherne's face, blinding her, choking her.

'What do you see?' Kay urged but gently now, still holding the girl.

'I see that I allow this.'

Aherne threw back her head and keened a desolate cry torn from the very depths of her soul. She rocked back and forth, her eyes closed tightly in pain and sorrow.

'My mind begins to shatter. I of all people in the land. To do such a thing. The horror. The horror of such betrayal. I of all people.'

'Why not you?' Kay demanded shaking her. 'Why not *you?*'

Aherne's eyes opened suddenly and stared straight into Kay's. But they did not glitter with madness as Kay so deeply feared. They shone with the light of clarity as all memory and knowledge flooded her mind.

'Because I am Eriu. The Rising Queen.'

★　　★　　★

They sat late into the night, talking in low voices as the fire crackled and burned with sweet scented wood.

'Aherne was my child-name before I came of age, before the rites of initiation and my tutelage as queen.'

'That's why you went back to it,' Kay said. 'When your mind broke, you *were* a child again.'

Kay looked at the girl beside her, noting the subtle change which had taken place. The green eyes still flashed with the innocence and rash spirit of Aherne, but there was also the quiet wisdom and unyielding will of a young queen trained to govern her people. 'The most promising ruler for generations,' Eolas the Chief Druid had said in the Brugh. She sat erect, as if the mantle of authority were already draped on her slim shoulders, and her voice echoed with the timbre of command.

'I misunderstood the vision of the *tairfeis* even as the Druids did. Indeed it would come to pass that I would love the enemy king,' and she smiled briefly at the thought of Amergin, 'but that is not the reason why I would allow the conquest. What both I and the Druids saw as betrayal is merely acceptance. The passing of the Danaan order is fated to occur. You have made that clear to me, Kay, from your knowledge of the future. And thanks to our quest I know why, though it leaves me bitter. My people have lost the sovereignty of Inisfail by their own misrule. Had we made peace with the Formorians and the Firbolg, we would not be a divided land prey to invasion.' Her features hardened with pain. 'Even if we fight the Gaedil, I know we will lose, for we cannot change what is to be. We must therefore accept the conquest to prevent needless bloodshed. It is the right thing to do.'

Though her voice was steady, her eyes grieved without hope.

'A poor destiny to see the end of one's race. It is a terrible time to be alive.'

Kay took her friend's hand as she nodded in sympathy.

'I know how you feel. That's what I've thought too in my own time. The war that's likely there won't destroy just one land but the entire world.' Kay's eyes dimmed with thought. 'I used to be frightened by the idea of the end of the world. Then I decided that since I couldn't stop it, the end itself wasn't as important as how I faced it. If I could continue to believe, to hope and have courage, I would keep a light shining against the dark. When all's said and done, isn't that what life is about?'

Kay's words seemed to comfort the girl as they both stared into the fire. Then Kay added in a lighter tone.

'We still have work to do, you know. The Sword must be won and the Stone has yet to be found. The quest isn't over even though you are queen.'

'Not queen yet,' the other girl replied with a laugh, then she was serious again. 'You will not treat me any different now, I hope. Are we still friends? And will you call me "Aherne" as you have done since we met?'

'Nothing has changed between you and me,' Kay promised. She grinned at Aherne's concern. 'I'm not impressed by your title. I know your bad side.'

The two burst out laughing and hugged each other with all the love of their friendship.

Then Aherne spoke quietly.

'I shall run this race tomorrow for the Sword and the sovereignty.'

Kay nodded in agreement but she looked worried.

'It's going to be dangerous. The Druids are against your succession.'

'Not all the Druids,' Aherne said, after thinking a while. 'Eolas, my foster-father, will not stand against me. If we seek his help and draw up our plans well, we can yet hope to succeed.'

Kay smiled briefly at the girl's assertive tone and realized that her own words were not quite true. Things *had* changed between the two friends. Aherne was now making the decisions as she moved into command. She was the Queen Rising.

'What's your plan?' Kay asked her.

Chapter Nineteen

Not accustomed to driving the chariot, Kay approached Tailltiu slowly. She was glad she didn't have far to travel. It was a struggle to control the movements of the car and the fierce tug of the horses at the end of the reins. But she was reassured by the presence of the two treasures hidden behind her.

Tailltiu was not a permanent rath of the Danaan people but a low-lying hill set in lush pastureland. It was the site chosen by King Lug in ancient times to hold the games that now marked his summer feast of Lugnasad. Kay remembered what Cahal had told her. The hill was named in honour of Lug's foster-mother, Taillte of the Firbolg.

Like a great outdoor fair, the lawns of Tailltiu were thronged with crowds. Silken pavilions shimmered in the sunlight. Carved stakes ringed the hill with ribboned banners. Spectators sat on rich mats strewn on the high earthen banks that overlooked the playing fields. The games had already begun: chariot races and sword play, horse racing and jumping, lines of warriors hurling javelins, and furious team contests with stick and ball. Both men and women wore short white tunics and competed in their bare feet for the collars of gold that were the prizes.

On the hill of Tailltiu itself, poets and singers and musicians strove to be the greatest of their kind. Stringed instruments echoed with melodious sound. Voices reached heights of ecstasy. Words were strung like pearls in rows of beauty. These were the *aes dana,* the high caste of artists.

Amongst the crowds wandered jugglers and acrobats, sporting fantastic masks and clothes of rainbow hue. Here and there walked Druids in black tasselled mantles, their faces composed in serious dignity. Warriors strode confidently in full battle-dress. Old men and women sat over board games with gold and silver pieces. Children played loudly, some swinging above their heads a wooden toy that whirled with a fluttery musical sound.

Kay listened to the tumultuous joy of the throng and admired the splendour of the Danaan people. Tall, light-eyed and fair of face, some had the burning copper hair of Aherne, more had tresses of honey-gold. They wore flowing raiment of silks and satins. Jewels sparkled on their throats and hair. Seeing their beauty, Kay felt a pang of regret that they would no longer rule Inisfail. Then she remembered Liag and the massacre of the Formorians, and Cahal and the hungry faces of his tribe. As if to confirm her thoughts she noticed everywhere the serving people: those who carried trays of food, who led horse and chariot for the Danaan lords, who waited silently for commands. All dark-haired and dark-eyed, they were a smaller race, the bound slaves of the once-free Firbolg. Kay's heart hardened. The Tuatha De Danaan were like the wealthy of her own world, shining and beautiful but thoughtless of those who suffered under them.

Kay kept her distance from the crowds all lost in the pleasure of the day. With hood drawn over her face, she searched quietly for Eolas. When she found a small tent set alone behind the hill of Tailltiu, she stood in the chariot and reached out with her mind. A few moments later, the door of the tent was drawn aside and Eolas stepped into view.

He seemed to have aged since the last time she saw him in the dark chambers of the Brugh. His face was grey with unhappiness and his eyes were dull and withdrawn. But curiosity brought life to his features as he gazed at her, a travel-worn stranger in her long green cloak.

'Greetings, wisest of Druids,' Kay said when he walked up to the chariot. 'We have met before.'

Awe and wonder kindled in his eyes. 'It was *you* behind the Sentinel's hedge. I sensed your power and a great distance in time and space. There was another with you,' he hesitated, hope mingling with fear in his voice. 'A younger girl.'

'You mean Eriu, your foster-child and the Rising Queen.'

The old man trembled but Kay had no time to spare him the shock of her revelations.

'She is in hiding not far from here and she needs your help. She's going to run the women's race to claim her sovereignty. Will you support her?'

Eolas's face darkened with the struggle of his dilemma.

'She has been condemned by the priesthood to which I belong. And she is outcast from her tribe.'

Kay looked at the Danaan people enjoying the games and then back at Eolas.

'I know it's a difficult position for you. But sometimes you have to stand alone against everyone else and do what you think is right. It's what another wise man told me. You must follow your instinct for the true.'

Eolas smiled with sudden humour and he seemed less careworn.

'I have lived long enough to know that I can learn from the young. I accept what you are saying. I shall stand with my beloved daughter.'

He brought Kay into his tent and gave her cakes and wine while she told him the story of the quest and the treasures. When she spoke of the invasion, he nodded with sadness.

'All the visions were true, then. The defeat of our race was rightly foretold and it is Eriu's destiny to preside over that end. Though it grieves my heart, I cannot say I am surprised. My tribe has acted wrongly for many ages past. As we laid low our enemies, so too we shall be laid low ourselves. It is hard justice but it *is* justice. What we inflict on others we must suffer in turn. The spiral of life demands it and I have always known that.'

'At least Aherne will prevent a war,' Kay pointed out quietly, 'and no one will die in vain.'

'But first she must rise to the queenship,' Eolas said. 'It will not be easy. This is a perilous place for her. She has no friends in Tailltiu. Her sisters Banba and Fodla have remained in Temair to express their anger at what the Druids are doing. But as their terms of rule have ended, they are powerless against the priest-hood. The Danaan people themselves know that Eriu is outcast and prey to the Sentinels. They will not support her.'

'The Sentinels!' Kay remembered with a sudden chill. 'Are they here?'

She was relieved when Eolas shook his head. 'They still ride the land in search of her.'

'Well, that's one danger we won't have to worry about,' Kay said pensively.

But there were so many others. To run the race for the Sword, Aherne would have to enter into the midst of her enemies. Kay fought against the fears that crowded her mind. She tried to concentrate on the strengths of their situation. There was Eolas the Chief Druid and Kay herself plus the power of the two treasures. And if the Sword was won that would strengthen them further.

'If she wins the race,' Kay asked Eolas, 'will she be safe?'

'The Druids have promised that the winner will be queen, but Fiss and Fokmar are cunning. And the priesthood are behind them, greedy for power. I am certain they will rise up against her no matter the outcome.'

'Then we'll have to reserve our power till the race is over,' Kay decided. 'We'll need it to set Aherne on the throne. That's what she has suggested herself. This is her plan: you and I will stand together against Fiss and Fokmar. We must ensure that Aherne is allowed to run the race. Whether she wins or not, she means to claim the sovereignty at the finish. This will not be easy, it may even be impossible, but the attempt has to be made. The treasures must be kept secret. They are not to be used till she states her claim to rule. There may be a battle. We will need all the surprise and power we can muster to support her.'

★   ★   ★

The women's race was announced when the sun reached its zenith in the sky. The heat and blinding light were to be one more obstacle added to the test. All other activities of the festival ceased as the Tuatha De Danaan gathered on the grassy banks of Tailltiu.

The air crackled with tension and excitement. The women's race was always the highlight of the games as it was run in tribute to the Goddess Danu. But on this day the contest was charged with more meaning still. The Danaan sovereignty was a term of seven years and succession normally flowed from Queen to Rising Queen. But she who should have risen was now cursed as traitor to her tribe. The Druids had proclaimed their solution to the problem. The women's race that honoured the Goddess would decide who ruled as queen in Her name.

A dais was raised at the summit of the hill and beneath its silken canopy was a marble table which held the Sword. The hilt of ivory and blade of diamond were bared for all to see. Beside the table stood Fiss and Fokmar in their dark-red gowns, eyes glittering with wily triumph. They were pleased that Eolas had agreed to stand with them as it showed unity amongst the Chief Druids. For this reason they had not objected to Kay's presence on the dais, though they eyed her with distrust. Eolas had introduced Kay as a Mage from foreign lands. Her blonde hair was piled high above her calm face. She wore the same dark robe as the Druids and a golden collar around her neck. Both Fiss and Fokmar were uneasily aware of the balance of power around the Sword, but they were too certain of their plans to fear disruption.

The Firbolg slaves had erected the last obstacles of the race-course which ranged around the entirety of the hill. The runners were at the starting point. Tall daughters of the Danaan tribe, they wore white tunics above their strong limbs and their yellow hair was bound in braids.

Kay looked down at them anxiously. Where was Aherne? Had Eolas's apprentice reached her in time?

A musician stepped towards the starting line and raised a curved trumpet to his lips. A blast of sound was the call to start and the women began their run.

Kay bit her lip as she watched the speed of the girls. Where was Aherne? Suddenly from the crowd, a slim figure stepped forth dressed in a dark-green cloak. Kay's heart lifted as the girl walked boldly to the starting line and tossed aside her mantle. She wore a tunic of emerald hue and her hair streamed like fire.

A ripple of shock ran through the spectators. Green was the favourite colour of the Rising Queen. Red-gold was her hair.

Eriu.

Her name was whispered through the crowd like a song on the wind.

She began to run, leaping over the first hurdles like a gazelle in flight. Her limbs were long and agile, every muscle strengthened by the days of her adventuring. The obstacles before her were conquered as if they were toys. The tests were nothing compared to the mountains she had scaled, the plains she had crossed, the great rivers she had forded. She bore down swiftly on her competitors. The breathtaking speed of her run, the fierce pride of her movements, the very courage of her appearance in that race swayed the multitude in her favour. Caught up in the emotion and daring of the moment, they started to chant her name, urging her on with fervour.

Kay smiled at Eolas with grim satisfaction. Things were going well. The Tuatha De Danaan might yet accept their rightful queen despite the indictment of the Druids. Kay glanced over at Fiss and Fokmar to see how they were taking Aherne's arrival. She sucked in her breath. Fiss had disappeared and Fokmar was glaring at her with open hatred. She could feel him probe her mind, the chill power of evil grasping with iron vice.

'Cease Fokmar!' Eolas's voice rang out. 'Or else we battle now. Let the race run its course.'

Kay saw Fokmar waver. She knew he was weighing the possibility of her own strength added to that of Eolas. Would he try to fight them now? With relief she felt him withdraw his hold. She didn't want to use her power or that of the treasures. Not yet.

The runners had disappeared around the back of the hill. Some of the crowd ran to watch but most stayed where they were, enjoying the suspense of awaiting the first to come into sight. But where was Fiss? Kay scanned the hill anxiously and then her heart stopped. Above the fair heads of the Danaan people, she saw three antlered figures with eyes cold as death. Fiss had called the Sentinels! Kay's face went white. The girl Aherne had been safe as a changeling child but now she was Eriu, their lawful prey.

Eolas stepped behind Kay and whispered urgently.

'You must hold the waves from the shore till the Queen can claim her heritage. I cannot command the Sentinels over Fiss and Fokmar.'

Kay was sick with worry. Their plans were upset, the timing all wrong. She needed her power to support Aherne if the girl won the sovereignty and more so if she didn't. Eolas couldn't be left to battle the Druids alone. But Kay could see the Sentinels moving towards the bend in the hill. Saw them draw their daggers. They wouldn't wait till the race was over. They would kill Aherne as she ran.

Mustering her strength with all the love she held for her friend, Kay reached out to grasp the minds of the Sentinels. This was the greatest trial of her powers she had yet to face. The Sentinels were untrammelled force, wild and elemental. It was like trying to gain mastery over the winds of the air, the storms of the sea, the upheaval of the earth. She had them in her grip but only barely as they struggled and fought. Their resistance was furious, explosive, shattering. Kay's mind began to break beneath the strain.

'Use the treasures,' Eolas insisted when he saw that she was fainting with her effort.

'Not . . . yet,' Kay gasped, still maintaining her hold. But it was slipping. She knew it was slipping.

The runners came into sight. A cry rose up from the crowd. *Eriu. Eriu.* She was out in front, her long hair flying behind her like wings of copper, her bare feet hardly touching the ground.

When the Sentinels spotted their prey, they surged forward with a last burst of defiance. Kay's hold was broken and her mind screamed in agony. Then she knew. She couldn't reserve anything for Aherne. The girl would have to manage her victory alone. Kay needed the power of the treasures *now*.

She drew on the Spear and the Cauldron as the Sword was not yet theirs. But it was enough. The rising flood of energy buoyed her mind and like a giant fist she clamped down on the Sentinels. They froze in their place, hands still poised in the air and daggers glinting in the sunlight.

Aherne saw them before her as she ran and for a moment checked her pace. But with a quick glance up to Kay on the dais she pressed on bravely, placing her trust and her life in the power of her friend. She passed the Sentinels unscathed and reached the finish as the Tuatha De Danaan roared ecstatically.

Chapter Twenty

Aherne lost no time in secur-
ing her win. She saw Kay fall to her knees on the dais, racked
with pain. She saw Fokmar reach for the Sword and Eolas
block his path. All the years of her training, all the courage and
will of her character, rose now to help her act with ingenuity
and speed.

'Queen's guard to me!' she cried.

Warriors ran forward in answer to her call. They hoisted
her on their shoulders and carried her through the cheering
crowd, up the hill and onto the dais. Pushing Fokmar aside, she
bounded for the Sword and raised it high above her head. Light
burst forth like an explosion of white fire.

'I am Queen of Inisfail!' she cried. 'Queen of the Tuatha De
Danaan!'

Throng-filled Tailltiu roared back its approval.

Unbalanced by the speed of her actions, Fokmar stared in
astonishment at the blinding light of the Sword. This had
never happened before. The blade of diamond had never
shone so brightly. Terror began to undermine his power as he
remembered the legends of the tribal past. And to confirm
his fear, Eolas was taking from their hiding place the Spear
and the Cauldron. As the three treasures hummed with
energy and glowed with light, Fokmar felt his own power

die. Kay began to revive as the Druid's assault on her mind ended.

'What took you so long?' Kay said weakly when the Queen bent down to help her to her feet.

'Not quite as we planned but good enough I think,' was Aherne's reply and she smiled at Kay with love and concern.

Still supporting Kay, the Queen issued orders swiftly to her guard.

'Take Fokmar and keep him bound. Search for Fiss. These Druids are traitors and I will deal with them later.'

Eolas was standing to one side, his face grey with strain.

'I am sorry I could not protect your friend, dear Queen. My mind fought a feeble battle with Fokmar.'

Aherne's eyes were warm as she looked at him.

'Wisest and most loyal Eolas, beloved foster-father. You did well. Had Fokmar taken the Sword nothing could have saved Kay or you and me. You acted rightly to stop him.'

Eolas brightened at her words and took Kay upon his arm.

The Tuatha De Danaan had grown quiet, sensing that some great drama was unfolding before them. They could see the three treasures on the dais and ancient memories were stirring in their hearts and minds.

Aherne faced her people, the Sword in her hand.

'Make way for the Sentinels!'

The crowd parted as the three giants strode forward. Their antlered brows towered above the tall Danaans. Their leafy cloaks rustled over the ground.

Aherne addressed them in a high and respectful tone.

'Lords of the Green Leaves, sons of Danu. I hold the Sword of sovereignty. In ages past, before the Druids wrested this right, it was the Queen who commanded you in the name of the Goddess. Will you accept a return to the old ways?'

It was Radarc who answered. As he glanced from Kay to Aherne both were certain they heard an echo of warmth in his voice.

'The events of this land do not concern us. We obey as we are called. But our minds are not dimmed by time and indeed it was the Queen who called us before the Druids did. We accept your command.'

Aherne smiled triumphantly. 'You will not regret that decision, Radarc. For I not only end your hunt now but I release you from bondage to my tribe. No more will the Sentinels ride on their terrible duty. You may wander as you will.'

It was as if the wind blew through the lofty branches of a mighty forest. A tremor of joy ran through the three giants and each bent silently on one knee, their antlered heads bowed low before the Queen.

'I have a last request,' she said quietly, 'before you leave the Tuatha De Danaan forever. Three journeys and three messages.'

'We will do your bidding gladly,' Radarc replied.

They rose to their feet and took their place beside her, a formidable honour guard. Aherne was pleased. She knew the effect such a sight would have on her people: the radiant treasures, the great Sentinels, two dark-robed Druids and she, the young Queen newly risen to her sovereignty. She counted on these potent images to buttress her words, for she was about to deliver to her race the news of their doom.

'Tribe of the Goddess Danu, I speak as your Queen, I speak as Inisfail. You know of the impending invasion of our land and I tell you now, it begins at sunset on this very day.'

Like a storm cloud crossing a sunlit sky, all faces turned towards her darkened abruptly. But Aherne gave them no time to react. She continued fearlessly.

'You are prepared for war, I know, but I say now *there will be no war*. Eolas, our Chief Druid, has seen in the bull-sleep that we will be defeated. So too have I. Nothing can prevent the conquest. I, sovereign of this land and law over you, have made my decision. No blood will be shed in vain. We will not fight. We will suffer a noble surrender not an ignoble defeat. I am Queen and I have chosen the path we will walk.'

She paused to allow her words to settle in their minds. She saw their confusion, the pain and sorrow, but no sounds of anger or protest were made. She stood in all her glory, surrounded by the symbols of her authority. They had no choice but to accept her command regardless of their feelings. Grief marked every face turned towards her and yet she could feel their assent. Her heart ached for her people but she stood unmoving, features stiff with resolve.

'Clear the main pavilion for a council,' she ordered. 'All Druids and leaders of war bands meet me there. The rest of you return to Temair and await word from your Queen.'

A pall of silence hung over all as the crowd slowly dispersed. Aherne turned to Kay.

'Can you stay by me? Are you well enough? This is the darkest hour for me.'

Kay nodded with wordless sympathy and said quietly, 'The third treasure is reviving me.' Then she added doubtfully, 'Are you sure they'll obey you?'

Aherne looked surprised. 'There is no question of it. Disobedience to the Queen is unheard of. It was different when I was the Rising Queen. For better or worse I now represent the Goddess in this land. I *am* Inisfail.'

The Sentinels had called their stags to the dais. The splendid beasts were pawing the ground with new-found freedom and impatience. The Queen gave her instructions to the sons of

Danu and they rode out from Tailltiu on their last service for the Danaan tribe.

Kay's heart thrilled as she watched them ride away, magnificent giants with antlers arching against the sky. She smiled when one halted on a hill top to wave his final salute.

'Goodbye, Radarc,' she murmured. 'You'll haunt forever the hills and forests of this land, an eternal image of all that is wild and free.'

Aherne's eyes too were shadowed with appreciation and respect.

'I remember now the legend that attends the Sentinels. They were bound by the Goddess to Her tribe only till our reign should last. This is one more sign that our end is near.'

The Queen walked heavily into her first and last council. All were assembled as she had ordered and Kay saw immediately that Aherne's words were true. There was no hint or trace of rebellion in the faces of both warriors and priests, only an air of defeat and utter sorrow. They waited in silence for the Queen to speak.

Aherne held her head erect and spoke with quiet command.

'The Sentinels are riding on their last duty for our tribe. Fiac to Inber Scene, Rusc to Inber Colptha and Radarc to Inber Slaine. As no others could, they will arrive before sunset and offer the invader our terms of surrender. I have asked the Gaedil to direct their fleets to the eastern coast three days from now. At the hill of Ben Edar we shall offer up this land to the new sovereign. In the meantime the Firbolg race will begin their trek across Inisfail to resettle the mountains and highlands of their former home. There will be no resistance.'

Aherne looked sadly around the room at the proud faces resigned to their fate. Her own eyes echoed their grief but she stilled her tears.

'It is your duty to carry this news to every hill fort and rath, every corner of Inisfail. Gather our people. March them to the east. Tell them to wear their brightest finery and to fly banners from every horse and chariot. Remind them of Lug and Nuadu, Brigit and Macha, the Dagda and the Morrigu. Bid them keep in their hearts the splendour of our ancestors so that the past will shine like a torch against the darkness of the future. Let our passing be marked with beauty and pride so that the memory of our people will echo in this land like the strains of an ancient song.'

There were no tears or protestations. Not a word was spoken, but a light shone in the eyes of all as they drew strength and inspiration from the words of their Queen. They would do as she bid. The last hosting of the Tuatha De Danaan would be a glorious one.

As the pavilion emptied, Aherne leaned on Kay, her tears flowing freely at last.

'Would that it were not I who had to do this,' she said in anguish, 'and yet I know I have done it rightly.'

'That's all you could do,' Kay murmured, putting her arm around her friend. Then she squeezed Aherne's shoulders. 'But it's not over yet. You worked hard for the third treasure and we've got one more to go. We're still on the quest. Let Eolas look after the hosting. You and I have another journey to make before you stand at Ben Edar.'

The old eagerness brightened Aherne's features. 'Where to now?'

'The Stone is waiting for us,' Kay said. 'We'll have to ask Fintan Tuan how to find it. Get your cloak, my girl. We're off again.'

Chapter Twenty-One

Kay and aherne scaled the precipice that led to Fintan Tuan's tower. The royal chariot had carried them to the base of the mountains and they had climbed the rest of the way on foot.

They were not the same pair who first came to Fintan blindly seeking his aid. Both wore clothes of Danaan finery beneath their broad cloaks. Aherne walked with the assured bearing of a sovereign, her long hair bound by a golden circlet. Kay stepped quietly behind her, content that her role as queen-maker had been fulfilled and eager to complete the last stage of the quest. After their many trials and adventures, neither had any difficulty ascending the peak of Ton Dubh. Both were fearless and strong.

When they arrived at the oaken door of the tower they found Fintan waiting for them. He did not wear his rough gardening clothes nor was he the fumbling old man who had greeted them on their first visit. Before them stood a wise and ancient figure in a fur-trimmed robe. Upon his breast shone a gold medallion with the sign of the triple spiral. An air of serenity suffused his features and his blue eyes gleamed like a sunlit sky, clear and ageless.

'Welcome, daughters, from your questing in the world,' he said solemnly. Then he bowed courteously to Aherne.

'Welcome, fair Queen of Inisfail,' But as if the moment of formality were over, his eyes twinkled. 'You have proper shoes upon your feet this time.'

The three of them laughed but Aherne's voice was surprised and almost hurt.

'Did you know who I was even then?'

'Indeed I did,' he said affably. 'But one does not tell the young what they must learn for themselves. My duty, like all elders, was to set you on the right path.'

'You certainly did that,' Kay said. 'We found three of the treasures. We couldn't carry them up here but they're safely under guard. We haven't looked for the Stone yet and we're hoping you'll advise us.'

'You have done well,' Fintan said. 'The most difficult part is over. The three treasures in your possession are calling to the fourth. Have you come to understand the purpose of the quest?'

The girls frowned thoughtfully at each other. Aherne answered first.

'I rose to be Queen and stopped a war.'

Kay nodded in agreement.

'And I discovered my power and used it to help her.'

'And I have been restored,' said Fintan, 'and so too is my hall. But that is just a hint of what the treasures can do. As I told you before the quest, it is when the four are united that their true power shines forth. The time has come for you to know what the treasures mean and why they were wrought.'

He opened the door of his tower and led them to his hall. They saw immediately that all had changed. What had been shadow and dust was now bright and alive. The fountain splashed vigorously, filling the air with a fresh sweet scent and the soft music of falling water. The marble sea serpents were no longer cracked and broken but gleamed with a wet and vibrant hue. It was the tapestries, however, which caught their eyes. Flowing upon the walls like liquid colour, scene after scene breathed with life and sight and sound. They could hear leaves rustling, oceans roaring, could see the very blades of grass shiver in the wind. And as great figures strode within the cloths like actors across a stage, the murmur of voices echoed through the hall.

'Wonderful work,' Kay said breathlessly. 'Living pictures of reality.'

'Oh no, daughter,' Fintan said. 'These are not pictures. This *is* reality. In my tower, all that unfolds in the passing of the ages exists here in unity, woven on the fabric of space and time. Here the past, present and future are one.'

He took each by the hand and sang out in a clear and powerful voice.

> *Here lies the wisdom of Fintan Tuan of True Knowledge*
> *He who stands beyond the reach of time.*
>
> *See you now the history of hosts*
> *Pleasant it will be*
> *Fair the rewards of knowledge*
> *To see the peoples bounteous, multitudinous,*
> *living, glorious.*
>
> *See you now the four cities of splendour*
> *And the treasures of power wrought within.*

They were glad that Fintan held them by the hand for this was the strangest journey they had yet to take. They weren't sure whether they had stepped into the tapestries or whether the many-coloured cloths had furled around them but in a moment of rushing wind and sound and chaotic colour, they were no longer in the hall.

They were walking in a cold land, they knew, as their breath streamed before them like mist but they could feel nothing, as if they were shadows treading the soft snowy ground. All was sparkling white with dunes and drifts of snow. Before them rose a city of crystalline beauty: archways and terraces fashioned from ice as if from opal; walls like a forest of blue pinnacles; white castles of frozen cloud and canopies of lacy frost; frazil floating in cool fountains. Overhead the sky was a silvery grey.

'This is fair Findias,' the old man told them as they entered the gate. 'The White City of the Hyperborean Lands.'

He led them through the glistening avenues to an open square where the city dwellers had gathered. Kay and Aherne gazed with awe upon the people of Findias. They were a noble race of high and stern majesty. Their features were lofty and uncompromising. Unshadowed by doubt or wrong, they seemed as pure as the white moon or the newborn soul.

Wide steps ascended from the square to a shining temple of pillared ice. All eyes were on the temple. A murmur of joy, like the soft sigh of snow, rose up in one breath as a figure appeared on the steps.

The King of Findias stood between the pillars, his fair hair bound back from a high forehead and eyes cloud-pale. In his hand he held the Spear, tall as he, with ivory shaft and diamond blade. Two lights shone with equal radiance, the blade of the Spear and the face of the King.

'Lug the Shining One!' Aherne cried. 'This *is* a Danaan city!'

Fintan nodded and spoke in a low voice. 'The Spear of Lug was wrought in the city of truth. It is an invincible weapon for no victory can be won against it. No matter its trials, truth cannot be overcome.'

Hands still clasped, they left Findias and found themselves walking on the sandy shore of an ocean. They could see people bathing in the blue-green waters, their faces brown from the sun and full of vigour and playfulness. In the midst of the swimmers, dolphins tumbled and splashed, fearless of harm. Not far from the shore was another city and the girls smiled with delight when they saw it.

It was a city of fantastic design and vivid colour. Turrets, towers and spiral chambers whorled in laocoon shapes, their masonry a profusion of the stuff of the sea; crusted conches with inner pale pink of shell; tiny cowries and smooth abalone; clusters of coral—yellow, apple-green, orange and deep blue; periwinkles, purpura and speckled cones. And dripping from each edifice like exotic gardens were the fruits and flowers of the waves. Shrubs and fans of sponge splayed their tentacles like translucent trees. Sea anemone flowered in bursts of pink and white. Jade-green seaweed dangled in long filmy strands. Everywhere was a riot of watery colour and the resonant sound of a thousand shells whispering the music of the sea.

A triton shell trumpeted its call and the swimmers left the ocean and moved with fluid grace into their winding city. Fintan and the girls followed the crowd into a spacious hall of mother-of-pearl. There in the centre of the floor stood the Cauldron, surrounded by tables where the people sat. Kay and Aherne were startled to see that the treasure wasn't empty. The bowl of ivory brimmed with fat lobster, pink crabs, oysters and shrimp all bubbling in a stew that splashed against the diamond rim.

Fintan chuckled at their surprise.

'The lively people of Murias wouldn't make a treasure for beauty alone. It is an unending well of plenty. See who presides over the feast.'

The throng in the hall were noisily awaiting their meal. Loud cheers greeted the huge plump man who carried a ladle over his shoulder as if it were a weapon. His cheeks were like rosy apples and his eyes crinkled with mirth but there was great strength in his features. He was obviously a jolly, bountiful King.

'Ollathar the Dagda,' Aherne said with a smile. 'He whom we call The Good.'

'The Cauldron of the Dagda,' Fintan told her, 'is the treasure of charity and generosity. No one leaves it unsatisfied.'

They were in good humour when they left Murias but now a fierce and awesome scene unfolded before them.

Red was the hue of the land and fire its element. The smouldering earth was a vast hearth covered with a film of ash that swirled like mist. Incandescent gases, white fumes and hot steam sprayed from faults and fissures like angry breath. In the distance, mountains erupted in volcanic grandeur, showering the dark sky with streamers of light. Amber clouds glowed like haloes. Lava flowed in molten rivers. And over the land crawled terrible creatures, dragons with sleek scales and salamanders hissing in the red night.

The girls walked with Fintan along a giant's causeway of lava stone and as they approached the third city both gasped with wonder.

'Fire-bright Gorias,' Fintan said but there was a frown on his wise face.

Before them was an immense citadel that glittered like a dark prism. The latticed structures of feldspar and obsidian were jagged and luminous, splintering with all the beauty and disorder of crystals growing in a cooling fire.

Dazzled by the sight, the girls followed Fintan into the heart of the city till they came to a wide black pool. Standing at the water's edge, bearing torches in their hands, were the people of Gorias. The flashing eyes, the proud and ardent faces reflected the turmoil of their land. All were adorned with hard metals and weapons.

To the dark tarn strode a giant of a man, hair red like flames and eyes fierce with pride. In his hand he bore the Sword, its diamond blade still glowing with new life. As he stooped to cool the Sword in the shadow of the waters, steam rose with a hiss to cloud its ivory hilt. The people of Gorias let out an exultant cry.

'The Sword was Nuadu's,' Aherne said with quiet recognition. 'The King from whom I am descended and the first Danaan to rule Inisfail.'

Fintan nodded and his voice was grave. 'Nuadu it was who forged the Sword of War. No one can escape its wrath, not he whom it is wielded against, nor he who wields it.'

'The one treasure we never lost,' Aherne murmured, her eyes dark with knowledge.

But there was no time to talk, no time to think for they were leaving Gorias and entering a new scene.

CHAPTER TWENTY-TWO

A GREAT AVENUE LINED WITH GIANT STAND-
ing stones stretched before them. The stones stood separate, stolid
and cold grey, like sentries guarding a sacred byway. Overhead the
sky shone a deep blue and underfoot the ground was a lawn of
green grass. Silence hung in the air like a heavy veil, and the air
itself was still as if holding its breath in anticipation. But it was
not an empty place and Fintan and the girls were not alone as
they walked. They were part of a shining company, a stream of
tall and beautiful people, all treading with quiet purpose.

'My ancestors!' Aherne said breathlessly, then she was silent
again as she felt her words disturb the calm.

She looked around her with wide-eyed excitement. It was
a homecoming for her, a moment of unbridled happiness and
satisfaction. Her heritage and ancestry, bounteous, multitudi-
nous, living, glorious. There was Brigit the poetess, her gentle
hands leading two white-shouldered oxen; and Niamh of the
Golden Hair, tear of the sun; Mannanan mac Lir, he who rode
his chariot upon the waves of the sea; Macha the horsewoman
and her shining Grey; Aengus the Ever-Young with his gold-
chained swans; and Iarbonnel the White, first poet and prophet;
and more and more. She knew them all. They were the bright
assembly, the Danaan pantheon, the long and radiant line of the
tribe of Danu.

Last Queen of the Tuatha De Danaan, Aherne who was
Eriu walked proudly in their midst, her own blood thrilling to
be one with them.

They walked for miles it seemed till they came at last to a
great stone circle. It was evening now as time ebbed and flowed
of its own accord. The sky's cloak had fallen, blue-black and
cloudless, eyed by the gaze of a dim red moon. The henge rose
up darkly, gargantuan stones capped one upon the other with
ponderous weight and solemnity. The space within the circle
seemed limitless as the assembly filed in, shining like candles.

Kay had remained silent throughout the journey but now
memory stirred in her mind. The stories in her books seem to
crowd around her, the stories set among the megaliths of the
lands of Europe. She turned to Fintan with a puzzled frown.

'This isn't a city.'

He gave her a wise look.

'This is part of a city,' he said. 'You may use your power,
Kay. It would not be wrong here.'

Her grey eyes dimmed as she gathered the force of her
mind and reached outwards. She saw the avenue they had trod,
the miles of pathway and thousands upon thousands of stones.
She began to tremble.

'Carnac!' she whispered. 'The stone lines of Brittany.' And
she stared with new eyes at the circle that surrounded her.
'Stonehenge! The same but not the same. This one isn't old.'

'Go further,' Fintan said with quiet encouragement.

As her mind ranged freely, Kay grew aware of every
dolmen, menhir and henge, every mound and cairn, every
temple and tomb raised up in the far-flung lands. A vast
network, a web of stone that stretched over islands, mountains
and plains. The megaliths. The building blocks of a city beyond
imagining. The City of Stone.

'All are Failias!' she cried.

And even as she returned to herself, she sensed the company around her, their minds open to each other and ringing with power. Mages all, this Danaan race who had raised the stone monuments to build Failias. A titanic effort. And yet, she sensed there was more.

Knowing her thoughts, Fintan spoke.

'See the fourth treasure which was the crown of Failias and Morrigu the Great Queen who was the Chief Artificer.'

Into the henge stepped a magnificent woman. Her gown shone like the evening sun, her hair like liquid gold, her eyes black as the night. Her face was a mirror reflecting the wisdom of the ages. She lifted her arms and began to sing. The others joined her and the stones of Failias echoed their song till it seemed that all the lands were a chamber reverberating with sound.

Kay felt the ecstasy of their song of power. These were the people who had raised the City of Stone with the power of their minds. And now they were calling the last formation into being—the heart-stone, the keystone, the Lia Fail. Before her eyes it took shape, building itself in the brilliant swirl of power, a massive archway, a fiery door.

'The greatest of treasures in the greatest of cities,' Kay whispered. 'The Singing Stone.'

When the stone stood complete, Morrigu's eyes blazed with triumph.

'The last treasure has been wrought!' she cried to the assembly. 'Bring the others forth to forge the link and let the Stone sing our destiny!'

The Kings of the three cities brought their treasures into the circle. The Spear, the Cauldron and the Sword were placed beneath the archway of the Stone.

Kay's mind swooned with the sudden burst of power, greater even than that which had been used to raise the Stone. She could feel the treasures joining together, each strengthening the other till their force spiralled upwards in a limitless chain of energy.

An expectant hush had fallen over the company and the silence was charged with overwhelming hope and desire. But though the treasures surged with power and though the Stone shone with inviting brightness, no song was sung.

A ripple of anguish ran through the Danaan people. Morrigu's triumph died in her eyes. A whisper sounded through the circle. Nuadu's name and then *the Sword*. There was no anger in that whisper, only sorrow and the terrible echo of loss from the core of every heart.

'Exile!' the Morrigu cried in pain. 'We are bound here!'

The Stone dimmed and so too did the henge and as darkness gathered to obliterate all, Kay and Aherne found themselves back in the hall of tapestries. Her voice shaking, Aherne echoed the grief and loss she had felt in that circle.

'We were like gods upon the earth.'

Fintan's eyes were dark as he looked at her.

'These were not human cities. You *were* gods.'

★   ★   ★

Their minds dazed by the visions they had seen, the girls stared at Fintan dumbfounded. Aherne recovered from her surprise with a determined effort.

'Please tell me what you mean, noble father,' she said. 'Many things have I learned since I last left your tower but it seems the greatest lesson is still to come.'

'All in good time,' Fintan said, placing his arm gently around her. 'Let us rest and eat and I shall tell you what you must know.'

He led them into the big warm kitchen and once again they drew their chairs to his hearth and shared the food of his table. But all had changed utterly. Their minds were ringing with the images of the tapestries and they waited breathlessly for Fintan to explain. At last he sat down with his pipe in his hand.

'In the earliest days of the world, and this is known in your time also Kay, gods lived upon the earth as well as men. The Tuatha De Danaan were such a race and their four great cities were their shining abodes.

'But as the race of men rose to take sovereignty over the lands, the gods began to depart from this world. Each race built its own bridge to cross over to the Upper Realms from which they came in the beginning and to which they ever longed to return.

'The four treasures were the bridge of the Danaan gods. Linked together, they would forge a chain of power to span this world and the next. The last and greatest treasure was the portal through which they would cross over. The Stone was to sing their destiny and open the doorway to infinity.'

Fintan grew quiet and the girls could see in his eyes the same grief which had resounded through the vision of Failias.

'They didn't pass through the door,' Kay said. 'The Stone didn't sing and they were exiled on the earth.'

'Because of the Sword of War,' sighed Aherne with bitter knowledge. 'It was the flaw in the diamond, the flaw in my race . . . the weak link in their power.'

Fintan nodded. 'Each treasure rose from the strength of your people, but the power of war weakened that of truth and charity. Thus it worked against your rightful destiny.

'It was a moment of utter defeat for the Danaan gods. They abandoned their four cities, accepting mortality as their doom. They set out in their fleets for the most distant island of the western world. Though they were glorious, skilled in all arts and capable of all things, it was in Inisfail that the Tuatha De Danaan began their slow descent. With each passing generation, the knowledge of who and what they were steadily faded. Their divine heritage was obscured by the mists of time and further darkened by their behaviour in the present. They lost two treasures to the peoples they treated so wrongly. They kept the one which had been their downfall. When they made it the symbol of their sovereignty, they brought upon themselves its curse of war and conquest. They forgot the Lia Fail, though Inisfail was named in honour of it, and the Stone has stood silent through the ages, abandoned, untried . . . *waiting*.'

Kay heard the change in Fintan's voice and the accent on the last word. Her heart beat quickly. She was about to speak but stopped herself, knowing that the truth was not hers to realize. But her eagerness burst out as she leaned forward to grab Aherne's arm.

'Do you see what he's—?'

There was no need to urge Aherne. She had clenched her fists as Fintan spoke, afraid to consider the possibility underlying what he said. But her palms ached with the ferocity of her hope and now she saw her own thoughts confirmed in Kay's eyes. She trembled fitfully as the tears ran down her face.

'The Sword of War was our downfall. And its wrath has kept us in exile from the Realm of the Gods, our rightful heritage. But now in their darkest hour my people have changed the Sword. We have chosen a different path from the one which led to our great failure so long ago. We have chosen peace over war, the divine over the mortal. It would seem,' and her words almost caught in her throat, 'that what I believed was our ultimate defeat is about to be . . . our infinite victory.'

Fintan's eyes were joyous as he bowed before her.

'I salute you, last Queen of the Tuatha De Danaan. Last and greatest. You have accomplished what your noble ancestors could not do. The link of power has been rightly forged. The Stone will sing for you.'

Her face shining through her tears, Aherne acknowledged his salute.

'This is a happy destiny. All difficulties and hardships are as nothing compared to this outcome.'

She began to laugh, a young and carefree laugh that signalled the end of all her doubts, worry and pain. The burden of rule was lifted from her and she basked in the sheer delight of a task completed and work fully rewarded. She had succeeded. Beyond all hopes! Beyond all dreams!

The other two laughed with her, a laugh of celebration and freedom.

Then Aherne smiled graciously at Fintan.

'I thank you for your guidance and wisdom. It was the quest which led me to choose the right path. But in truth, I could not have done it without Kay.'

The girls grinned at each other with wordless happiness and Fintan's comment caught them by surprise.

'Naturally, daughter. I chose Kay for that very purpose. She was the . . .'

He stopped speaking when he noticed Kay's startled look. He frowned as he stared into her eyes, searching for something that he couldn't find. It was his turn to be surprised.

'Have we had our talk yet?'

Kay was confused. 'We spoke late at night before I went on the quest, when you told me I had power. But I still don't know . . . I mean, I haven't found *my* answers.'

She heard the disappointment in her voice and struggled to control it.

Fintan smiled kindly. 'You and I have one more talk to come. I thought we had it already but I'm confusing time again, I'm afraid. *Don't give up,* as you have been telling Aherne all along.'

In the silence that followed, Aherne took Kay's hand and the two sat staring into the fire. Finally the Queen spoke, her mind returning to her people and their approaching fate.

'The Tuatha De Danaan are meeting the Gaedil at Ben Edar to offer up the land of Inisfail to the new race. How can I find the Stone and take it there?'

Fintan's face wrinkled with amusement.

'The Stone is destiny. You cannot go to it. It comes to you. Take the three treasures when you ride to Ben Edar. The fourth will be there. You have woven your thread in the tapestry, great Queen. Your quest is over. Let the future which already exists unfold before you.'

CHAPTER TWENTY-THREE

THE SUN HAD BEGUN ITS DESCENT BEHIND THE height of Ben Edar which loomed over the eastern coast of Inisfail. The Tuatha De Danaan were gathered on the terraced slopes. From the steep cliffs up to the broad summit they stood, tier upon shining tier of men, women and children. Arrayed not in battle-dress but in cloths of gold and silken mantles, they glimmered like the eyes of a peacock's tail fanned out across the mountain.

Before them spread the sea, a sheet of pale blue laid out beneath the clouds. And upon the waters sailed the Gaedil fleet, great ships of skilful design and grace. From bow to stern the conquerors thronged the decks, golden torcs at their throats and swords sheathed in bronze.

All was still, suspended in the calm, as the two races looked upon each other, the old and the new.

On the summit of Ben Edar stood a massive dolmen, arching against the sky with stern grey majesty. In the shadow of the Stone, two figures watched and waited, both cloaked in green.

'I have chosen the way for my people,' Aherne said quietly to Kay. 'Let us see how they follow it.'

A ringing sound echoed over the waves as the Gaedil unsheathed their swords. Metal flashed as red as blood in the sunset. Skilled in the arts of war and science, the Gaedil were ready to do battle if the surrender went astray.

The Tuatha De Danaan saw the glinting weapons and didn't flinch. Hands linked in a great chain along the coast of their land, they began to sing. Their voices rang with the power of their heritage and the skills of wizardry that marked their tribe. They called on the wind and the waves till both rose in a tempest of unleashed freedom. The air howled in cyclonic gusts. The sea heaved like mountains. It was an awesome sight, nature answering to the call of the Danaan race, and the Gaedil wavered. They knew this power was far greater than their own.

'The storm will destroy the fleet,' Kay said, as the Gaedil ships were tossed and pitched like apples on the waves.

'It could,' Aherne agreed.

A slight smile played at the edges of her mouth as she listened to the proud song of her people.

Kay gave her a quick look of suspicion and worry.

'If there is treachery, Queen, your race will be banished forever from the Upper Realms.'

Aherne's face was bright with mischief.

'It is but a little joke I am playing on my arrogant prince. At this very moment, he strides about his ship, cursing loudly.' She burst out laughing, then added in a calmer tone, 'Do not be disturbed, Kay. No one will be harmed.' She tapped her head lightly. 'My people and I are one. We are already moving towards our immortality. They hear me even as I speak to you and I have allowed them this last song of grandeur. Listen now and I myself shall lead the chorus.'

As Kay looked out at the storm-tossed ships of the Gaedil, she heard Aherne's voice rising over the roar of wind and sea.

I am the tribe of the Goddess Danu,
I am the people of the cairns and mounds.
I am a Spear that pierces truth not flesh,
I am a Cauldron of feast and plenty,
I am a Sword mended by peace,
I am a Stone that sings of destiny.

I am the people of art. Who but I sets the cool head
aflame with fire?

Who but I looks from the great dolmen arch?

I am Eriu, Queen of the Tuatha De Danaan,
I am Inisfail, Land of Destiny.

Come forth, Prince of the Gaedil,
You who claim the right of sovereignty.

Be swift and cunning and together we shall sing the final
incantation.

As Aherne sang, the storm increased in ferocity. Thunder and lightning shattered the sky. The Gaedil fell to their knees with awe. This was not a human race before them but a shining celestial people. This was not the race of Inisfail but the *gods* of Inisfail.

There was one among the Gaedil who didn't kneel, for he recognized the voice that sang to him. Amergin stood upon the prow of his ship, mantle billowing behind him in the raging winds. Defiantly, he ignored the storm as his eyes settled on the tiny figure far above on Ben Edar.

'Aherne!' he called and his voice was carried to her on the wind. 'Change as you may, *I claim you*. It is my right. You cannot escape me.'

When she heard his words, Aherne laughed with boundless amusement and Kay laughed as well to see her so wild.

'He says I cannot escape him,' the Queen cried, her eyes dancing. 'Then we shall have a chase, he and I.'

She stretched out her arms to touch the Stone and called on the power of the fourth and most potent treasure. Once again her voice sang out to the Gaedil.

> *Come, Prince, and meet me*
> *In the Land Upon the Waves*
> *And we shall harvest the apples*
> *That are under the sea.*

The voices of the Tuatha De Danaan were suddenly quiet even as the storm itself died in a moment of utter stillness. The sea swell lowered in the pale light of dusk. The tattered sails of the Gaedil ships fell limp as the wind stopped, but though the fleet was disabled no one was hurt. The Gaedil recovered from their shock and leaned weakly against the sides of their vessels; for a great marvel was taking place on the water beyond them.

There upon the sea, leaping over the waves as if it were dancing in a forest glade, was a lovely fawn with a hide of red-gold. It raced playfully with the foaming crests and jumped high over the rushing hollows, its tiny hooves prancing with delicate step. And the eyes of the fawn were green like water. But the dance didn't last long. Over the sea sped a savage hound, white as alabaster, with ears flattened against its head in the fury of the hunt. The points of the ears were tipped red like blood but the eyes were a dark-brown.

The pursuit began in deadly earnest. The fawn fled swift as the wind. The hound bore down, lean and hungry, fangs bared for the kill. But just as it seemed that the hound would catch the fawn, the gentle creature began to waver like the waves, to change its form. It grew and expanded, the red-gold coat now glittering with scales. Its hooves were sharp talons and from its long curved mouth, flames spouted forth. The crimson dragon flew into the sky and hovered over the hound. As it lowered its claws, the great wings beat the air like thunder.

'Bravo!' Kay cried, delighting in the spectacle and the spirit of the game.

But her shout of glee was short-lived for now the hound too changed its form. Moving in the sea was a winged serpent with gaping mouth and skin like armour. Impervious to the sharp rake of talons, the serpent coiled its white body around the dragon and pulled it from the sky. The battle was terrible to behold. Wings beat and battered, coils twisted and strangled, fire burst forth and the sea boiled. With titanic rage they struggled together till both sank below the waves.

Silence hung over the water. Both Gaedil and Danaan waited anxiously in the calm.

'Aherne!' Kay cried. 'Amergin! Yield to each other. You must yield!'

The anxious seconds seemed like hours, until with relief Kay saw movement in the depths. Up from the sea rose a lovely woman clothed in a gown of green. Her red-gold hair fell to her waist. She rode a grey horse that trod upon the waves. And even as the Lady had risen from the sea, so too did another rider. His steed was jet-black, the colour of his mantle, and around his throat shone a golden torc. There was but a moment when the Lady looked upon the rider and her face lit up with surprise and laughter. And the dark man, his eyes settling on her, laughed too with the joy of the chase. He reached for the bridle of her horse before she could flee and his voice was triumphant.

'Change as you may, you cannot escape me.'

He threw back his head and answered the challenge of her song.

>*I am the Gaedil of the blood-dark battle host*
>*I am the people of free companions.*

>*I am the torc of gold, brighter than the sun*
>*I am the hero's light, the flame of courage on the brow*
>*I am fir flathemon, prince's truth.*

>*Through me*
>*Darkness yields to light*
>*Sorrow to joy.*

>*I am a breaker threatening doom*
>*The boar-champion, ruthless and red*
>*I am the tomb of your hope.*

>*I am the son of Milidh, Prince of the Gaedil*
>*I am Amergin, King of Inisfail.*

His song of victory sounded over the waves and reached his people in their battered ships. A jubilant cry rose up from the Gaedil.

Upon her shining horse, Aherne bowed her head towards Amergin and her red-gold mane fell in a cloud over her face. But when she tossed back her hair, her eyes showed neither remorse nor grief.

'The Lia Fail, the Stone of Destiny, grants your claim. The sovereignty is yours, young King. Land your ships. My people are leaving Inisfail for evermore.'

Chapter Twenty-Four

KAY SAW THE LADY BOW TOWARDS THE KING. The final incantation had been sung. The conquest of Inisfail was complete.

The Gaedil ships sailed into the harbour just north of Ben Edar. The conquerors kissed the soil of their new homeland as they came ashore. Bonfires of celebration flared in the darkening night. Already tales of the Tuatha De Danaan were being told around the fire, tales of the gods and goddesses of Inisfail.

Even as Amergin had returned to his ship, Aherne was back beside Kay on the summit of Ben Edar. The Queen's eyes sparkled like emeralds.

'A game well played and a song well sung,' she said to Kay with a lively smile. 'He will be a good King. But now it is time for the Tuatha De Danaan to depart.'

She raised her hand in a signal to Eolas. The Chief Druid brought the three treasures to the Stone. As he laid the Cauldron, the Spear and the Sword beneath the great archway of the dolmen, Eolas's face was bright with joy. The same joy shone in the eyes of every Danaan as they looked upwards from the slopes towards the summit.

As the four treasures stood together, Kay was overcome by the surge of power that she had felt once before in the vision of Failias. But now the four joined together without flaw or weakness. Ivory to diamond and diamond to stone, the power of each treasure linked with the next till their energy spiralled endlessly. Power enough to bridge the distance between the finite and the infinite, to span the chasm that lay between one world and the next.

The Stone began to glimmer. A blue-white fire seeped through its form and increased in intensity till it blazed like a star. And it seemed to grow in size so that its archway was immense, a silver bow to challenge the arc of the sky. From the portal's depths came exquisite music, a wordless song, unworldly melody. It reached out across the mountain towards the race of Danu, calling and beckoning, inviting and promising. And with the waves of music, light issued forth as if a door had opened onto the fiery plains of the sun.

A cry rose up from the Danaan gods. They recognized the music deep within their hearts and they knew its source. With speechless joy, they ascended the slopes and moved towards the Stone. They were leaving the land of their exile and returning Home.

Kay and Aherne stood quietly by the Singing Stone as the last hosting of the Tuatha De Danaan passed in procession beneath its arch.

Two dark figures approached them, limping as if in pain.

'Greetings, Chief Druids,' Aherne said, as Fiss and Fokmar bowed before her.

'What is your will, great Queen?' Fokmar asked heavily.

He glanced at the shining portal with fear and longing.

'You who once gave judgements, what do you expect?' Aherne said sternly.

'Death or exile,' he answered in a flat tone.

Aherne nodded, but she spoke in a gentler voice.

'Greater than you have fallen among our race but all will pass through. In the infinity of time, none shall be robbed of their inheritance. Seven years you will remain in Inisfail. Instruct the Gaedil in the Druidic arts and knowledge. Teach them the history of the Tuatha De Danaan who will be their gods. When you have completed this task, you may pass beyond.'

The two Druids bowed low and left with a happier tread.

'A good judgement,' Kay said.

Aherne smiled wisely. 'Their power is greatly lessened and they will work no mischief if they wish to join us. The Gaedil will benefit from their knowledge.'

When the last of the Tuatha De Danaan had passed through the Stone, its voice grew quieter and its light began to dim. Kay and Aherne stood alone on the peak of Ben Edar. In the distance glowed the fires of the Gaedil camp. Around them hung the black shadow of night.

'I have to go now,' Kay said with sudden realization. 'I came through the Stone to get here and it's the only way to get back.'

The girls looked at each other with pained surprise. All the rush and excitement of the adventure had always veiled this moment and now they faced it unprepared. They had never spoken of a parting, never thought of a possible end to their companionship.

'It is not right,' Aherne whispered. 'We have come through so much together. All that we have suffered and accomplished should bind us forever. Why are you leaving me?'

Kay shook her head bewildered.

'I don't know. It doesn't seem fair to me either. But we don't belong together. We come from different places. There's nothing we can do about that.'

Aherne's eyes filled with tears. 'I do not have the words to say how I feel about you. To do it properly, Kay, as a Danaan I would sing you an endless song of praise. You were my hope, my strength, my . . .'

'It's not fair,' Kay said, through the tears that blinded her. 'You're the first person I've ever been close to in my life. My first real friend. And I'll never see you again!'

They clung to each other as if they would never let go, tears mingling with strands of hair, eyes dim with grief.

Then Aherne stopped crying suddenly and placed her hands on Kay's shoulders.

'Who says we cannot meet again?' she demanded. 'I am a Goddess. You are a Mage. Who could stop us?'

Though her face was still wet from weeping, Kay couldn't help but laugh at the girl's defiant logic. The two grinned at each other with power and determination.

'Agreed,' said Kay. 'We *will* meet again.'

Strengthened by that decision, Kay stepped towards the Stone. As she stood within the shadow of the archway, she turned to her friend.

'What about you? Are you going to stay?'

The Queen drew back against the black sky, her cloak swirling in the cold wind of night. Her long hair flew wildly from a pale and tragic face that showed her torment.

Caught up in that moment, neither girl was aware of the slight figure who made his way up the slopes of Ben Edar, driven by a reckless fear and urgency.

Aherne looked towards the Gaedil fires and back to Kay.

'This is the part of my destiny most difficult to accept.'

'There are choices within destiny,' Kay said. 'Again and again in the pattern, the choices were yours. You've been making them since I got here.'

'I am Queen. I must follow my people,' Aherne said unhappily.

'You are Inisfail,' Kay said. 'You have a right to stay here.'

Aherne shook her head blindly.

'I will pass behind you.'

Kay's heart ached for her friend but she knew the decision was Aherne's to make.

'Try to be happy,' Kay whispered.

But even as she raised her hand in one last goodbye and even as Aherne moved slowly to follow her, a great cry reached them.

Amergin had reached the summit. His mantle was torn from his headlong ascent and his face was white with fear that he might be too late. He saw first the Stone and Kay standing beneath it, then Aherne who was only a short distance away.

His voice rang out, furious and yearning.

'Don't break our pact, Aherne!'

He strode towards the Queen and caught her up in his arms. Her red-gold hair fell over his face and shoulders as he lifted her high against the stars of the night.

'Don't break my heart, beloved.'

From the shadow of the dolmen, Kay saw Aherne's arms encircle Amergin like a halo and the whispered words reached her in the Stone.

'I will stay.'

Kay smiled as she remembered. 'That was in the stories too. The Goddess weds the King. The ancient law of sovereignty in Inisfail.' Then she corrected herself. 'In Eriu. He named his new land in honour of her—he was the first King of Eire.'

CHAPTER TWENTY-FIVE

KAY WALKED THROUGH THE PORTAL OF THE Singing Stone, expecting to arrive back in the Wicklow mountains where she had begun her odyssey into Inisfail. But instead of the wet ground of a rainy mountain and the fresh air of the Irish hills, she found herself in a different place altogether.

It was like stepping into the heart of a wind chime. She was surrounded by pieces and edges of glass, a splintered kaleidoscope that tinkled with sound.

'What's this?' Kay thought. 'Isn't the adventure over?'

She felt a rush of excitement. After all her work on the quest, would she now receive her answers? Would the Stone give her what she sought? Was her own destiny part of its song?

She waited patiently, unable to move from where she stood. There were no pathways in the shining glass around her. She was trapped in the centre of a diamond, a crystal drop, a sliver of ice. The light and the music played around her and she looked curiously at the sharp angles of glass.

'They're a bit like mirrors,' she thought to herself. 'Maybe if I use my power . . .'

She had no sooner opened her mind when images took shape in the glass before her.

She recognized the scene. It was her first night in Inisfail. She and Aherne sat at their camp fire by the edge of the forest.

The younger girl, so tiny and frail, was staring at Kay with fearful awe.

'Are you a Druid?' she asked.

Even as the question sounded from the glass and reached Kay where she stood, another image took shape. Kay on the dais at Tailltiu beside Fokmar and Eolas. She wore the dark robe of the Druidic priesthood and the collar of gold around her neck. Her face was tense with concentration as she used her power to command the Sentinels.

'Am I a Druid?' Kay thought suddenly.

The image faded. Another rose to take its place. Liag of the Formorians, tall and silver-haired, glaring at Kay.

'Are you a sorceress?'

As if in answer to that question, Kay saw herself standing in the stern of a Formorian ship. With the shining Spear in her hand, she called on a power that could move wind and water.

'Am I a sorceress?' Kay wondered in the heart of the crystal.

The next image made her smile with sadness and joy. Cahal stood before her, his strong features appraising her.

'Are you a Mage?' he demanded.

Then Kay saw the two of them at the Cauldron Pool and her own mind strengthening his as he dived for the treasure.

'Perhaps that is what I am,' she told herself.

She remembered her stories. It was always the Mage who helped kings, queens and heroes. As if following her thoughts, the glass shone again and she saw Aherne standing on the peak of Ben Edar. The Queen's cloak swirled in the wind, her voice rang with emotion.

'You were my hope, my strength, my . . .'

'Is this the answer?' Kay thought, overwhelmed by the images and the message they imparted.

A final scene took form. Fintan Tuan's dark kitchen and a candle set on the table. The old man was hunched in his chair opposite Kay who sat dressed in blue jeans and sweater.

'And what am I?' Kay was asking him.

But now Kay was no longer watching the image. She was sitting at the table in Fintan's kitchen. With shock and disbelief, she touched the wooden surface in front of her and looked down at her jeans. She was certainly there. It all felt very real.

Fintan was staring at her through the flame of the candle.

'What do you see when you look at me?' he asked her.

For a moment Kay was completely disoriented, then with an effort of will she took hold of the situation.

'I've already answered that question, Fintan.'

His old eyes widened with surprise.

'You have?' he said and his look was puzzled. 'Have you already gone on the quest, then?'

Kay nodded, suppressing a smile, but it wasn't necessary as Fintan began to chuckle.

'Ah,' he said, shaking his head, 'the difficulties of not living within time.' Then he frowned suspiciously. 'Are you absolutely certain? You haven't just come down from your room where Aherne is sleeping to ask me what you are?'

'No,' Kay said, unable to stop herself from laughing. 'That was before. Now—this particular now, I mean,' and she was growing confused herself in the attempt to make it clear to him, 'I came through the Singing Stone and was looking at some mirrors. And you were in one of the mirrors and then . . .'

Fintan's face cleared and he laughed too.

'All right. *Now* I know where we are.'

He sat looking at her expectantly and at Kay's baffled silence, leaned forward to prompt her. 'Come, come. Ask your question. I can answer it in this now.'

Trying to be serious to suit the moment but giddy with humour, Kay asked with a grin, 'Well, what am I?'

Fintan smiled back at her.

'If you came through the Hall of Memory—the mirrors as you call them—your own memory, I might add, then you already know. A Druid, a sorceress, a Mage. There are many different names but they mean the same thing. Someone with special gifts and powers. The last name is the best I think. Appropriate to what you've been up to, helping kings and queens and what not.'

Kay nodded slowly. Yes, she had already figured that out for herself. Disappointment crept over her. A sadness she couldn't explain. Was that it then? Was that the answer she was seeking? But why wasn't she satisfied? Why didn't she feel happy?

Fintan's look was kind.

'You didn't ask what you really want to know. The more important question. Ask it now and I shall answer it for you.'

Kay's heart began to beat wildly and her throat tightened so that she could hardly speak. But she finally managed the words in a whisper.

'*Who* am I?'

Fintan's eyes glowed like dark pools of shadow.

'Look into *my* memory,' he said in a low and powerful voice.

Afraid but also eager, Kay reached out with her mind to enter Fintan's thoughts. The images she found flowed together like a story.

Aherne and Amergin were there, the King and Queen of Eire, in their great palace at Temair. They were in an airy bower that was bright with tapestries and scattered with toys. Both looked a little older as they bent over a golden cradle that held a baby. The child's fingers had reached up to catch Aherne's curls. Amergin was trying to untangle them as the Queen cried,

'Naughty!' All three were laughing and seemed to shine with happiness.

It was late at night. A dark wind blew through the silken curtains of the bower. The child's nurse didn't move to shutter the windows as she was fast asleep in the world of dreams. A black shape appeared at the open casement. A great hawk with eyes that burned like coals. It flew into the chamber and hovered over the cradle, then took hold of the baby with its deadly claws. A beating of wings, a raucous cry of triumph, and the hawk flew from the palace, bearing away the child.

Higher and higher the creature flew, over plains and mountains, and cliffs and sea. As it rose into the clouds that swept over the ocean, it was lost in a swirling silvery mist.

Kay followed the hawk's journey with the power of her mind, already grieving for her friends and the tragedy which had struck them. She was beside the hawk—no, just beneath it—as the clouds parted below them and the towers of a city came into view.

Kay's thoughts began to shatter as she recognized that city. It was the one where she lived. The one she had grown up in. She was already withdrawing from Fintan's mind with shock, when she felt herself being laid down upon the steps of the orphanage.

In Fintan's kitchen, Kay sat back with stunned disbelief. When she spoke at last her voice was hysterical.

'You mean my friends are my parents? *I'm Aherne and Amergin's daughter?*'

Fintan nodded without speaking and waited till Kay could recover. It took all her effort and will to finally reach a point of calm. Then her eyes narrowed as she glared at the old man.

'You are the hawk of time. You told me so yourself. Why did you kidnap me?'

'Isn't that obvious?' Fintan said quietly. 'Didn't you read the books I sent you? I put everything in those stories to prepare you for what lay ahead. There were several, I'm sure, about children stolen from their cradles—spirited away to come back much later and save the fortunes of their house or city or land.'

Kay stared at him dumbly. Though his words made sense, she was still too shocked and angry to respond.

The old man sighed and shrugged his shoulders. 'In all honesty I had no choice. When I was working on the last corner of the Danaan tapestry, I saw that your mother, Queen Eriu, was in great need of help. To fulfil her destiny and save her people, she would have to find the four ancient treasures of the Tuatha De Danaan. I hadn't the heart to send her on such a great quest alone and I asked the Goddess Danu if I could weave a Mage into the story. Once permission was granted I had to find one. There are a lot of them wandering in and out of time, but no one looked suitable.'

Fintan sighed again and shook his head at the difficulties of his job. 'I almost chose Merlin. It wouldn't have been too much trouble shifting him from Britain to Ireland and not that many centuries in between . . . but he has a penchant for younger women as you know from your books. I didn't like the idea of him traipsing around the countryside with the young Aherne. What I really needed was a female Mage.'

Even as he spoke, Kay found herself surrendering to the logic of his explanation. And in the back of her mind a little whisper was sounding its own notes of gladness and hilarious assent. She's my mother! All that time, I was helping my mother! No wonder I loved her so much!

'I had already begun work on the Gaedil tapestry,' Fintan went on, 'as it follows after the Danaan cloth, and I saw that the first child of Eriu and Amergin would be a great Mage herself.

It was cheating a bit, but it was obviously the answer. I stole a thread from the Gaedil and wove it into the Danaan. Quite appropriate, actually, since you belong to both races.'

'The thread you stole was me,' Kay said slowly. 'But why did you bring me into the future?'

'I had to put you somewhere,' Fintan said reasonably. 'Time was irrelevant since you had to "come back" before you were born, if you see what I mean.'

'I think I do,' Kay said, somewhat dazed.

Fintan's voice was gentle.

'It wasn't too hard on you, I hope? I couldn't let you grow up with your parents and then go back and help them. It would have confused matters too much and interfered with the quest. And if you remember from your stories, a Mage must spend time lost and alone and seeking. It's an essential part of your training.'

Lost in thought, Kay murmured her agreement. So much to think about, but it was quite wonderful all the same. She smiled at Fintan.

'Thanks for the books. They did help me a lot. But what do I do now? Where do I go now?'

Fintan beamed at her and waved his arms expansively.

'It's up to you. You are finished your apprenticeship. You are now a Mage as powerful as all your forebears—Circe, Morgan, Taliesin, Merlin. "The world is your oyster" as someone once said or will say.' He leaned toward her confidentially. 'If you don't like the time I placed you in—and I can't say it's one of my favourites but it was convenient for our purpose—why, you can choose another. Or move around a bit, spread your wings.'

Kay burst out laughing. 'It's like winning the lottery! I think I'll go back where I came from and put some thought into it.'

'Very wise,' Fintan said approvingly. 'Your power comes from your mother's side but you are certainly your father's daughter when it comes to practicality.'

Kay was suddenly wistful.

'Will I ever see them again?'

'Of course!' he exclaimed. 'Haven't I made that clear? All time is yours. As a matter of fact, by my knowledge you have already visited them on numerous occasions and have had great adventures.' His eyes crinkled with ageless humour. 'The time aspect is unsettling at first but you'll get used to it. You balanced it very well on the quest.

'You lost your childhood with your parents, Kay. That was the price of your power, a sacrifice which was necessary to help your mother. But you met them in their youth, something children don't get to do and they are now your friends to visit whenever you want.'

'That's a fair exchange,' Kay said with a satisfied nod.

The candle on the table had burned low in its dish and the flame flickered in warning that it was about to extinguish. Kay could see the kitchen wavering as Fintan's form began to fade. She knew that the Stone was reaching the end of her song.

'Thank you for everything,' she said to Fintan. 'As my mother said to you also, this is a happy destiny. All the difficulties and hardships are nothing compared to the outcome.' She reached out to clasp the old man's hands. 'And I'll see *you* again. Because I want to and I can. Isn't that right?'

Fintan roared with laughter and squeezed her hands. 'Of course you will. You're my favourite Mage. I'll be calling on you again when I need you. You can count on that.'

CHAPTER TWENTY-SIX

KAY LEANED OUT THE WINDOW OF HER apartment to look down on the paved courtyard below. The leaves of the oak tree had begun to turn brown and a few were already floating on the surface of the pool. The autumn breeze was cool and dry but it carried at its edges the chill hint of winter.

She closed the window and gazed thoughtfully around her room. Her own happiness was reflected in the changes she had made. The walls were freshly painted in vivid colours to match the Persian carpet that brightened the floor. Her shelves were lined with books of ancient wisdom and magic, with a special place reserved for the ones Fintan had sent her. She had a new stereo and music from many countries in the world. Antique instruments and ornaments were strewn over her new furniture. On a brass hanger on the door hung her green cloak with golden spirals.

Kay smiled at the cloak as she returned to her desk and her work.

'Almost finished,' she thought with a thrill of excitement. She flipped through the pile of handwritten papers. 'Not bad for a month's work and a kid who never finished high school. My mother's will and my father's brains, I guess.'

As she settled the papers in proper order, she glanced at the postcard which leaned against her jar of pens. A sunny scene of white buildings and bright exotic flowers. She turned the card over to read it once again though she knew the words by heart.

Dear Kay,

Don't know if you're back yet but I was homesick for Malta. See you late September if the Sirocco winds don't kill me. Couldn't find a postcard of the temples but will bring a photograph. Hope your trip to Ireland was successful.

Fond regards,
Alan Manduca

'As if I'd forget his last name,' Kay thought with a grin.

Her disappointment had been great when she returned home to find him gone, but when the postcard arrived her doubts were dispelled.

'Any time now,' she said happily as she started on a fresh piece of paper.

Later that day, the knock on her door sounded. In a moment of panic Kay considered not answering, but then she hurried to the door, forcing herself to be calm.

Alan stood in the hall looking very tanned from his holidays, with an open-neck shirt and faded blue jeans. But despite the modern clothes and his clean-shaven face, it was Cahal's dark eyes that regarded her with warmth and intelligence.

'Hello,' they said together and then laughed awkwardly.

'You cut your hair,' Alan said. 'I like it. You look different altogether.'

'Thanks,' she said shyly, running her hand through the short blunt cut. She wore tight jeans with a colourful T-shirt. 'The haircut makes me feel stronger and it reminds me . . . of a friend of mine. Um, would you like to come in?' she asked, realizing that he was still standing in the hallway.

'Hey, this is great!' Alan said, glancing around her apartment. 'It all looks new. Did you win the lottery while I was gone?'

'Sort of. I picked up some of my inheritance. Gold mostly, but it was enough to let me quit my job and buy a few things.'

Alan's eyes widened with excitement. 'So you found your family? Tell me about it!'

'I will. I promise,' she said, laughing more easily now. 'But first you have to tell me about your trip. I did all the talking last time. It's your turn to tell me things.'

'You *are* stronger,' he said with a mischievous grin. 'I just got here and you're bossing me around already.'

That sounds like something Cahal would say, Kay thought with amusement.

Alan sat on the couch while Kay made tea and toast in the kitchen.

'You remembered,' he said when she brought out the tray.

'I have jam but no biscuits,' she replied with a grin. She sat on a cushion on the floor. 'Your trip?' she prompted him.

'Wonderful!' he said, waving his hands expressively. 'I love my country! You will have to go there one day . . . but to start at the beginning.

'I completed the work on my thesis late in July and I wasn't looking forward to a long summer here with none of my friends around.' He gave her a look as he said this. 'So I wrote a sad letter to my parents, and just as I had hoped, they sent me a ticket home.' He burst out laughing, then added quickly. 'They can afford it, I assure you. And August in Malta! Perfect! Except for the winds I mentioned in my postcard. Did you get it? Good. The Siroccos come from the Sahara Desert but by the time they cross the Mediterranean and hit Malta they're murderously wet.

'But aside from them, I enjoyed myself immensely. Wandering around the island, visiting all the villages, celebrating the fiesta of Santa Maria. You'd love that, Kay. Processions and music and fireworks . . .' His face was bright with memory. Then he shook his head. 'When I first came here, I thought I'd stay. Now I know it's impossible. I couldn't live in exile forever. I've decided that when I have finished my doctorate, I'll go back to Malta and put my Political Science to good use. For my land and people,' he said with a self-conscious smile.

'You'd govern well, I'm sure,' Kay said seriously. Her eyes lit up. 'You're not thinking of growing a beard are you?'

'How did you . . . ?'

She refused to explain though she was in fits of laughter.

'It's a private joke,' she said, still chuckling. 'Did you bring me a photograph of the temples?' she asked, changing the subject.

'I did,' he said though he sounded reluctant, 'and I brought you a present too.'

'Well, where are they?' Kay asked lightly but then she noticed he was embarrassed.

'I, uh, haven't unpacked them yet,' he answered finally. 'I just arrived back a few minutes ago and . . . came straight over here.'

'Oh,' said Kay and her face matched the colour of his.

'Nothing like being obvious,' Alan said to the ceiling.

'It's okay,' she said softly with a little shrug. 'I mean, I feel the same way. I'm supposed to go back . . . home . . . for a while but I wanted to see you first. So I waited for you here.'

'I'm glad you did.'

Both were shy and formal as they acknowledged each other's feelings. They knew something important was forming between them.

'I went to visit one of the temples,' Alan told her, 'I thought of you all the time I was walking there. Hagar Quim it's called, the Ancient Stones, a great palace of rock that overlooks the cliffs and the sea. I imagined that I was a king in ages past and you were beside me, a noble lady.' He burst out laughing. 'I'm an incurable romantic.'

'Me too,' Kay said with a grin. 'That sounds very real to me.'

They couldn't help smiling at each other.

'So are you going to tell me the rest of your story?' he asked.

'It's a long one.'

'That's what you said the last time,' he reminded her, 'and we have all the time in the world . . .'

'All the time in the world,' Kay agreed with a laugh. 'But it is a long story. So long, in fact, that I decided to write it out.'

'You're kidding me!' he said but then he noticed the clutter of paper on her desk. 'Am I in it?' he asked jokingly.

'Yeah, you are,' she replied. 'You're at the beginning and the end. You're in the middle too but you have a different name.'

She moved over to her desk and picked up the sheaf of papers.

'It's not really that good,' she said, frowning nervously. 'There's a lot more work to be done and my spelling is terrible. But it's a good story.' Her face brightened as she smiled at him. 'It's just like the ones in the books I told you about.'

Her smile suddenly faded and she gave him a long look.

'I wrote this for you, Alan, and if you read it you'll know why. But if I let you read it, do you promise to believe it? Because if you can't or won't believe it, then . . . you'll never understand me.'

He could see that she was deadly serious and he had the strange feeling that some great decision was being placed before him. He looked at her slim form, the thoughtful face and grey eyes. Those eyes and their peculiar, far-seeing glance. Something told him that she was more than she appeared to be and that he would have to become more if he wanted to know her.

'I promise I shall believe it,' he said gravely. 'I'm willing to give you my heart and my trust.'

'You *are* a romantic,' Kay said with relief. 'And I promise to help you unpack when you've finished the story.'

She handed him the manuscript and sat beside him on the couch. He put his arm around her as he began to read.

HISTORICAL NOTE

For those of you who read *The Druid's Tune* set in Iron Age Ireland, *The Singing Stone* is a journey into the deep past of Cuchulainn's tribe, a tale of his Gaedil ancestors and the Danaan gods of his people.

History and myth are vague about when the Tuatha De Danaan ruled in Ireland. Many scholars maintain that they never existed at all. However, I have set their last days in the Bronze Age circa 1500 B.C. to correspond with the demise of the acropolis of Los Millares (near Almeria) in southern Spain. I believe that this is the city from which the Milesians, the sons of Milidh or Míl, sailed for Inisfail. But again, some scholars don't accept the legends that say the first Celts in Ireland came from Iberia.

I have changed the legend here and there to suit my story but for the most part names and places are taken from the *Lebor Gabala,* The Book of the Invasion. Written down in Old Irish possibly as early as the eighth or ninth centuries A.D., this book records the ancient pre-history of Ireland which had been passed down through oral tradition.

All debates aside, as someone once said, 'If this isn't how it happened, it's how it should have happened.'

Read more by

O.R. Melling

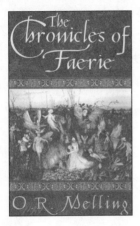

Entering the land of the Faerie brings magic, beauty, and special responsibilities. Join O.R. Melling's heroines as they brave the kingdom of the fairies in *The Hunter's Moon, The Summer King,* and *The Light-Bearer's Daughter* collected in The Chronicles of Faerie.

The Hunter's Moon

Findabhair and her cousin Gwen have always believed in magic and the other world, and their dream is to find a way to enter it. Where better to begin than at royal Tara, seat of the High Kings of Ireland? Eager for adventure, they challenge an ancient law by spending the night in the sacred Sidhemound. When Gwen awakens, she is horrified to discover that Findabhair has disappeared, abducted by the King of the Faeries. How will Gwen rescue her cousin?

The Summer King

Seventeen-year-old Laurel Blackburn has come to Ireland to escape the sorrow of her twin sister's death in Canada. After a magical experience involving her sister, Laurel's grandfather tells her the Irish once believed that Faerie was the land of the afterlife. Then a cluricaun, of the Clan Leprechaun, gives Laurel a mission: To help her sister enter Faerie, Laurel must find the lost King of the West.

The Light-Bearer's Daughter

Dana's broken family is about to immigrate to Canada from Ireland, despite her protests. Then the King of Faerie charges her with a mission: She must carry an urgent message to his second-in-command deep in the mountains. Why has he chosen Dana, and what has it to do with her long-lost mother?

Penguin Group (Canada)

Visit **www.penguin.ca/melling** to read an interview with O.R. Melling!

I n a landscape of Canadian myth and magic, the fairy tale continues . . .

Dana of *The Light-Bearer's Daughter*, now thirteen, has been in Canada for two years and she still hates it. There's no magic! Life gets even worse for the depressed teen when she finds her gateway to Faerie—her only escape from the misery of grade 9—mysteriously shattered. In a dream, her fairy mother tells her that all the portals to Faerie have been destroyed and that it's up to Dana to find *The Book of Dreams*—the key or secret that will re-open the worlds. The biggest surprise to Dana is that the magical book is to be found somewhere in Canada!

Can Dana quest in her new country the way she did in Ireland? Can Gwen of *The Hunter's Moon* and Laurel of *The Summer King* protect her from the dark forces that seek to destroy her? And how does Jean—a handsome fifteen-year-old Québécois classmate—figure in the mysteries that are engulfing Dana and the world of Faerie?

From Cape Breton to Vancouver, from Baffin Island to southern Ontario, Dana discovers the spirits of her new land and finds that Canada is home to magic as frightening and wondrous as anything she left behind in Ireland.

Penguin Group (Canada)

Visit **www.penguin.ca/melling** to read an interview with O.R. Melling!